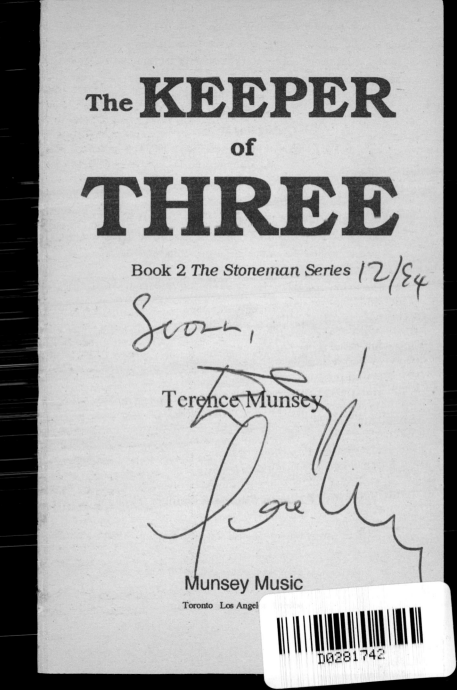

The KEEPER

of

THREE

Book 2 *The Stoneman Series* 12/84

Scott,

Terence Munsey

Munsey Music

Toronto   Los Angel

This book is entirely a work of fiction. Any resemblance to actual people, places, events, names, incidences, living or dead, is totally coincidental. This work is entirely the product of the author's imagination.

THE KEEPER OF THREE

published by:

Munsey Music

Box 511, Richmond Hill, Ontario, Canada, L4C 4Y8

Fax: 905 737 0208

Canadian Cataloguing in Publication Data

Munsey, Terence, 1953-
  The keeper of three
(The stoneman series ; bk. 2)
ISBN 0-9697066-1-8
I. Title. II. Series: Munsey, Terence, 1953-
The stoneman series ; bk. 2
PS8576.U5753K4 1994   C813'.54   C93-0952908-1
PR9199.3.M85K4 1994

Library of Congress Catalogue Number 93-86550

First Munsey Music original softcover printing   1994

Cover design, back note and illustration art © 1994 by Terence Munsey

Manufactured in Canada

Books by Terence Munsey in
The Stoneman Series:

THE FLIGHT OF THE STONEMAN'S SON

ISBN 0-9697066-0-X

LCCN 93-93660

Book 1

THE KEEPER OF THREE

ISBN 0-9697066-1-8

LCCN 93-86550

Book 2

LABYRINTHS OF LIGHT

(publication date 1995)

Book 3

Available at your bookstore

Acknowledgments

Thank you for all your help and encouragement:

Wendy Silverberg for proof reading and editing the final manuscript.

Christina Beaumont for the first proof reading of the laser 'camera ready' document.

Dr. Peter Terp for the final proof reading of the laser 'camera ready' document.

All of your many hours and comments are appreciated.

Make your journey a fine one. Not in beginnings or endings, but in everything between. The rights of entrance and passage are not ours to control. We exist in the middle zone. The real land of make believe.
Goodbye old friend!

Chapter 1.

"What a shambles this place is in!" Darla had hoped to find Julian awaiting them, in his garden with tea, just as before when all this turmoil had begun. It was about the same time of late afternoon as the day when she had first flung open Julian's garden gate with a loud clang and greeted the three astonished Jardians with her '*order*'. The words still echoed in her ears.

All the way down on the return trip to Jard, after the conclusion to the short lived Gott invasion, Darla had been encouraging and positive in her response to Eruinn and Thiunns' constant queries as to the whereabouts and safety of their Uncle. Not that distraction had been a problem! So many were now on the northern routes. The Jard Guard were everywhere re-establishing a presence. Replacements were coming up to the North and those whom had seen some action were being relieved. It would not take long to bring the area back to normalcy.

"Who could have made such a mess?" Eruinn continued, as the three stood looking at the small cottage where their journey had first begun. It had been such a picturesque and original place; everything was precise and orderly, but now it had broken windows and its front door, ripped from its hinges, was lying on a slant to the left side of the entrance.

"Lord Merm was behind this," Darla spoke with certainty, "It was good we started when we did. The *Evil* wasn't far behind." She now felt relieved that in the beginning she had permitted the nephews to accompany herself and Julian. "We were lucky. We must have missed the doers of this by a hair!"

"Lucky? Something still feels out of place here," Eruinn spoke pensively. He was sensing something, but couldn't quite understand what. As he continued, he tried to better explain his inner uneasiness. "I can't quite put my finger on it, but this is not right. No other cottage in this area appears touched in any manner. That's odd, isn't it?" he looked to Darla for confirmation, "What should we do? Just wait for Uncle Julian to arrive?" Eruinn was completely exhausted and unable to put the energy into explaining his situation.

Darla noticed Eruinn's uneasiness and in a more comforting tone added: "We need to rest and gather ourselves before planning further. I had hoped to find Julian here waiting for us. Hopefully he will have some answers when he arrives. This isn't finished yet." Darla was surveying the property as she spoke. She was worried for Julian though she did not voice her concerns, not wishing to upset the nephews. She also felt the slight uneasiness within her being, but like Eruinn couldn't understand the source.

Thiunn was only half listening while Darla talked with Eruinn when, without conscious thought, he decided to go toward the cottage. Something within his being was also gnawing away. He was curious about the condition of the inside and for some reason felt that Darla and Eruinn were overlooking an important fact. There was a strangeness here, or maybe it was just that he hoped to find his uncle mumbling away, tidying up the clutter that was everywhere! This confusion was too intentionally designed to be a random break in. It wasn't likely that Gott Troops had traveled this far. This type of rampage gave rise, in his mind, to many more questions; but these thoughts were left unanswered as he continued to approach the front doorway of his Uncle's abode!

"The war with the Gotts was over but..." he carefully thought about these things, as he walked into the cottage. He was being drawn, pulled ever deeper within the depths of the darkened home. He walked on into the cottage. Just as he was entering the room where he had left the note at the beginning of this adventure, there was a sudden feeling of chill. All the hairs on his body were pulling tight and standing up. He felt a presence. He was being watched. It was very disconcerting! There was the idea in his mind, of a raspy slither of a voice. It sounded old and tired. It was asking about the Key. It wanted the Key Give it back! It is mine! Who has dared to take it? Where was the other? Where— suddenly Thiunn turned and yelled.

"**Get out!**" He felt cold and shivery, and began to growl out his words to something he felt was there threatening, but not yet visible: "**Get out!...*Ici Ni Ban yi*.**" He heard himself uttering these strange words; they were in the language of the Old Ones. He wasn't sure what they meant, but knew they were words of power. He switched back to his own tongue, "**Get Out!...**" But the *Evil* would not move. It seemed to grow and confront him, energized by his fear. It was about to overwhelm...

After the routing, it was decided that the Gotts would make their way out of the South and disband their units. The Guard would supervise the operation. In the disorganization that now existed amongst the defeated Gotts, time was needed to find someone of leadership capacity to negotiate terms to officially end the skirmish. It was rumored that Lord Merm had perished. Nothing could be confirmed! There was so much chaos, as well as exuberation, for many of the Troop had never cherished the idea of a conflict with the *viscous* Jard Guard. There had been so many differing emotions running throughout the Gott Troops in the initial invasion against the South. Why was it so critical to invade the South? Had not the recent peace been beneficial to both sides? As a result, their conviction to fight was not very strong, especially since the Southern abilities seemed to have been greatly underestimated!

Tosh had been captured soon after the Old Ones had spoken. It had been during those last few moments of the routing of the Troopers by the Jard Guard. Tosh was standing upon a raised piece of farmland, calling out to the Troop to stop and regroup, when what he thought was a hand had been placed upon his right shoulder. As he turned to see to whom the hand belonged, all he remembered seeing was a bright circular glow and the vague image of a face. No sound was uttered. The shock of this apparition, combined with the panic of the routing, was all that was needed to push Sub Field Commander Tosh over the edge! He turned and ran off, eventually to be rounded up with the rest of the stampeding Troopers. Interestingly, only the Gotts had heard the voices of warning and only they were affected by their Magic; no-one else. The Jardians believed the routing of the Troops from the North, was simply the result of a well executed plan. No thought went to the yet unspoken explanation from the point of view of the defeated. They would never be questioned on the voices of the Old Ones that only the Gotts had heard, and the Gotts would never verbalize what they assumed had been heard by all and was therefore obvious to all! The Troops all respected the power of the Guard to cause such a feat! This was such an unanticipated occurrence, that even Area Chief Mal, who was still caught up in securing the situation, had never considered the possibility of the intervention of the 'Magic of Old', which surely, if he had had a notion, would probably have brushed off as an impossibility. Belief in the Old Ones was only myth and childrens' tales—certainly admitting belief in this type of phenomena was not worthy for a member of the Guard!

Gradually the Guard was rounding up the remaining Gotts and regaining control over the area. It seemed too easy a process—but no-one could afford at this point the luxury of stopping to consider the reasons. The Guard just felt the urgency to complete their mission to secure the area. They still half expected something— *anything* to happen and cause their foray to go astray, causing the complete demise of the South! They pushed on hoping that whatever was the cause of their present good fortune, would continue just a little longer

By the time the Guard had eventually stumbled onto a retreating and panicked Gott Commander amongst the rabble of Gott Troopers, the certainty of their success was beginning to sink in. A new strength and confidence was growing within each member of the small contingent of Jard Guard. The Gott prisoners were searched and separated, and Tosh was brought to the headquarters at the Inn to be questioned.

Tosh had begun to calm down after his capture and began blabbering about the voices he had heard. Mal and his men thought he was going mad from the trauma of the Gott defeat and paid little attention to his words. Tosh offered no resistance and was cooperative. His crazed chatter was easily written off during the moment. There were still more important matters to see to and dealing with this Gott's hallucinations was low on the current priority list. No time could be spent on such foolishness.

Mal tried to imagine a situation that would explain Tosh's state of mind. His dress seemed very convincing, yet at the same time Tosh acted far too unnerved for someone of the experience of this station. What would cause a veteran to 'lose it', if this Gott really was of the rank that his uniform suggested? One could never trust the Gotts, regardless of their apparent dress—it might be a ploy of some kind! This one Gott Trooper might have been planted on the rise by the *real* Commander in order to fool the Guard, and allow the *real* Commander time to flee back to the safety of the Lake. Of course Mal and his unit had no way of knowing, and so remained in doubt as to the verification of *this* 'Gott' as a Commander. Mal started his interrogation of Tosh.

"Who are you! Is this your rank?" Mal questioned brusquely.

"Tosh. Sub Field Commander, Seventh Division, and you sir?" Tosh was settling down.

"Area Chief Mal. I'm in charge of this unit. You and your Division are my prisoners. Do you agree to a total surrender?"

"I don't think we have any other option, do you sir?"

As Tosh spoke he indicated the mayhem that was clear in all directions. The Gotts were totally caught unaware, and had been routed. He was not stupid. There was only one option available: he would try to get the best terms he could under the circumstances. There would be no other help. He would be on his own in his decisions and without any guidance from his superiors.

As he sat he briefly wondered how all this was going to affect his future, if there was one; if that was the way things worked out. *How would Commander Citol or for that matter Lord Merm, react?* He knew he would not be able to remain in the South, they would not want him. After this was resolved he would either become a mercenary living in the Ice Barrens, or try to pick up whatever pieces were to be found in Norkleau. In any case, this present defeat wouldn't look good on his record, and it was too late to be concerned over such a matter. At least he hadn't deserted his duty as so many others had obviously done! He recalled the sight of Frid pilloried outside, and was happier to be in this type of position. It might be better received by the Gott Command. It certainly was less dishonoring! He shrugged it off.

"I am in your hands, sir. We," meaning his Division, "will take your orders until a formal understanding is reached. I am merely a Sub Field Commander, and not a diplomat empowered to negotiate such matters."

"Empowered or not, you're here and the highest ranking Gott that we've found yet. I'm afraid you will have to learn to play the role. Choice is no longer an issue, if you would like a rapid and compassionate end to all this. The longer we wait the more lives will be lost." Mal opened his arms to indicate the sight of the battleground as he spoke. "I cannot speak for the safety of the Gott troops once the local inhabitants begin to grieve and decide upon revenge." Mal smirked, knowing his point would be taken.

Tosh understood. The attack of the Gotts had been unfair and brutal. Revenge, especially against the leaders of such an invasion would be sought. If Tosh wished to endure this defeat, he would have to deal quickly with whatever hand fate's cards had dealt him. He had not yet realized that the number of Guard here abouts was small, and that they secretly wanted a settlement before the truth of the actual situation here at the border, was revealed to the retreating Gott Division. Even now the Gotts would be able to regroup and accomplish their original goals, if they were aware of the realities. Mal wanted a bargain that would end this invasion before all sides reassessed and started to dicker and apply leverage. He had the advantage over Tosh only as long as Tosh felt outnumbered and surrounded! There was a pause as Tosh considered his reply. Then believing what his eyes showed him, he said:

"Area Chief Mal. On behalf of the Gottlands, let us put an end to this fight. We request your terms."

They both shook hands, sat down and proceeded to negotiate. The Gotts would go home with a negotiated truce as opposed to an official loss. Tosh, though bewildered as to the reason, was relieved at this outcome. Out of a battle that was lost, from his present standpoint, came the glimmer of something won!

Mal hoped the deception of the small force of Jard Guards would last well after the discovery of the actual events. For now, both sides were pleased.

- - - - - - - - - - - - - - - - - -

"What was that! Coming from inside!" Darla's tone was sharp. Eruinn and Darla looked to one another, and for the first time noticing Thiunn's absence, blurted in unison:

"Thiunn!"

Darla, with Eruinn close beside, rushed into the cottage to discover the reason for all the commotion. As they entered they carefully went down the main hall following the sounds that grew louder till they reached the small bedroom. There, the sight of Thiunn fending off an invisible force was extended to them. It had the countenance of an unfairly matched arm wrestling contest. Darla drew her Jewel, and much like the episode in Norkleau, Jewel threw out a series of tremendous multicolored beams all hitting and absorbing into the opaque cloud of energy about Thiunn. Eruinn began hissing like a wild animal. He was unconsciously preparing for a powerful conflict. While all of this was happening and without warning, the consciousness of the *Evil* changed. There was a sudden comprehension of its being outnumbered and within the time it would take to snap two fingers, Thiunn had fallen exhausted to his hands and knees. By this time his two comrades, of whom he had been unaware of entering the room to come to his aid, had arrived and now stood beside him. The *Evil* let go its grip—the combat ended! Thiunn was dazed and in an awe filled state of silence. He began taking a subconscious account of himself. It had been a close call! It had all occurred within moments. As he slowly calmed, becoming aware of his surroundings, he gazed up at Eruinn and Darla, and short of breath, noted:

"If it's all over...and we're so 'lucky'..." he repeated the words of Darla, that had been said upon first seeing the state of Julian's cottage, "What was all that?...If Merm and the *Evil* are searching this hard I ...they must still be on the trail of Uncle Julian. Where is Uncle Julian? He must still be in trouble. He needs us. We'd better find him before...that, does!"

As Thiunn spoke, they each began to appreciate why Julian had disappeared from them without good-byes. He had not wished to expose them to the danger that would be following him. It was also evident that time was needed to get away, before the Key was tracked and he, along with it, returned shackled to this *Evil*. There was a knowing pause of silence. All of the three pondered on what was to follow. They realized that the battle with the Gotts had been won, but the war with the *Evil* was far from over. Their journey was not over, it was just beginning, again. This time however, there would be more magic and power between them, their apprenticeship being successfully completed. This increased power would cause more notice of them within the Balance. They now could be more easily tracked by the *Evil*. Ironically, their own growth and reawakening of their magic could now be used against them.

"How could that *thing*," indicating the *Evil* energy that had now totally disappeared, "have followed us here so soon? Why would it have followed us and not Uncle J?" Thiunn had a point.

Darla's thoughts brightened. Clearly Julian was still on the loose or the *Evil* would not have revealed itself so haphazardly! The Key and the *Passwords* must still be in the Stoneman's sovereignty. Darla felt a slight advantage. It would seem that the *Evil* did not yet know who had the Key and Books and where they were. There were many mysteries to solve. Julian was clearly not harmed, but enroute to his destiny. They must discover his whereabouts and also try to anticipate the next battle with the *Evil*. It was not going to be as easy as their last encounter in Norkleau and would require the strength of the few *Chosen* to bring the final ending. Darla accepted again the urgency of finding and protecting the Key with the *Passwords of Promise* before the *Evil* did. That was going to be difficult, since Julian carried them and had disappeared. Where was Julian? How were they to discover the direction of his flight?

"Well...our travels are obviously not over. There is not much time separating the *Evil* from us. We will have alot to discover if we are to find your Uncle and protect the Balance from destruction. In this victory against the Gotts, the worlds will not recognize these newer dangers. They will not be able nor will they want to assist us. We must act quickly! We must act *now*!"

"*Now*? But we just got back, and what of Mother? Can't we at least let her know we're alright?" Eruinn showed his irritation.

"You can go to her, but we mustn't waste too much of the time we have. Don't spend long and don't speak to her about your Uncle or our travels. Make up a believable story. She will be safer not knowing any secrets, in case the *Evil* seeks her out. While you are gone, I will look around Jard and find out whatever I can. Meet me here later this eve. You mustn't tell your mother of our plans. Think of her safety!"

"OK. We'll see you soon." Thiunn was recovering.

"Don't be late. You have been chosen and must complete your destiny. No one will be safe until we find your Uncle. Remember, not a word." Darla put a finger to her lips indicating a tight silence. It was understood. Eruinn and Thiunn ran off toward home. There was a new sense of urgency amongst them!

As they left, Darla placed her hands upon her hips and sighed, she was disquieted by the adversity that lay ahead. Overlooking the mess she decided to take a quick walk around. Some clues might still be lingering. There would not be much rest tonight, and then in the morning the beginning of another journey, and on to wherever it would lead them. She prayed they would arrive in time to find Julian before the *Evil* and Merm!

- - - - - - - - - - - - - - - - - -

After the routing of the Gotts, word had quickly spread throughout the area. It would not take long till all the South was aware of the conclusion to the threat from the North. In every village there was celebration as the news spread. Everything happened so quickly. Rumors also spread with the news. There was talk of the whole confrontation as a conspiracy, orchestrated by the leaders of the various regions for their own political benefit, some leaders being worried as to the outcome of the upcoming challenges to their office. It was unbelievable that these leaders could have staged the whole event, but it did appeal to the malcontents who acknowledged how certain incumbents would be hard to beat after such a successful campaign! The talk swept through the area. Villagers debated back and forth on every issue. These opinions would be discarded in time.

Jard was also quickly making plans to continue the Summer Festival, now that many would be returning to their homes, and in joyous spirit! To some, it seemed that all the threatening danger that had so quickly passed, was nothing more than just a bad dream; a dream that they were now all awakening from, soon to be consoled by caring parents. They would make up for the fear and lost time. The rapidly re-organized celebrations would lighten their moods and follow in the finest of tradition!

Sergeant Zer seemed to be the only one who questioned the ease of the win against the Gotts. Nobody concerned themselves with the 'predicament' that had, but a very short while before, struck everyone as hopeless! He consigned these thoughts to a corner of his

11

mind; the immediate reality necessitated attention. He decided to question more later, after things had returned to normal. There were many errands to see to. Amongst them was his promise to send word to Lenore of any news of her two sons the minute hostilities were finished. Somehow he had not expected it this soon. Everywhere was filled with jubilation and the difficulty in asking after missing persons at this moment forced Zer to consider a trip to Julian's cottage, to investigate himself. You never know, just in case they had come back unnoticed. If there was sign or word he could dispatch a letter to Lenore in the morning. It was near the end of his shift, so he decided to walk over and see tonight. It meant only a slight detour from his usual way home. Picking up his case he closed the door to his office and headed for the stairwell that led to the outside.

"Goodnight," echoed throughout the burnished stone walls as he left. Zer was respected and liked. These recent emergencies had shown the community his abilities and qualities while under the greatest of weight. He had remained calm and composed, giving the feeling of security to the panic of the others.

It was warm as he exited the building, the sunlight just beginning to wane. Trees were in full blossom, their aroma filling the slight summer breeze. As he walked, the sensation of the soles of his leather boots rubbing against the hard dirt path, helped him to relax. Taking in a deep breath, Zer felt pleased he was living in Jard and even more delighted that peace here reigned supreme. Now his new family could prosper in love and the peaceful nature of this place.

Everyone he met was more cordial than usual in their greetings as he traversed the path enroute to Julian's. Some were busy carrying parcels and preparing for the reopening of the Festival; others were just chatting and stood good-naturedly by the pathway. He was a hero in their eyes and had now risen to higher status in the community.

Eventually he veered off to the right and down the path. In a few more steps he would be outside Julian's sturdy stone cottage. As the dusk fell, he noticed that this part of the village was more dark and vacant than usual. He stopped, pulled out a hand lamp, then continued along. Not many inhabitants had yet returned from their temporary evacuation. It would take a little longer. By tomorrow that would all change and more would return now that it was truly secure. In this twilight world the Sergeant became anxious. The present ghost town appearance of these cottages along this particular path was spooky, causing him to fidget. His senses heightened along with his imagination. It was always fascinating how being alone can create such trepidation! Zer was not the type to feel like this. After all, he had spent his whole life in the service. This sudden development in his personality was alarming—something was up! His veteran senses were heightened!

He quickened his pace as if he was testing to see or hear another's increased hidden walk following. There was nothing. Julian's cottage came into view. Straining to make the place out, Zer began to notice the flicker of a light. *Had the Uncle returned?* Lenore would be overjoyed, and then be mad as...

"That's odd?" he spoke, as he thought, out loud. It soothed the uneasiness, "Why just one little flicker of light? Surely if they were back..." he pondered... "there would be more life and light," he assumed a possibility then abruptly changed to another, "unless..." he never finished the words, for as he neared the property, his hand light displayed the damaged door torn from its hinges and lying against the left side of the entrance. He remembered its thick dark wood as being standing and affixed when he was last here. In fact, the cottage looked like the victim of vandalism. A window had also been smashed. Again the effulgence, there was definitely a light coming from within. He saw the shadows of whoever was inside flicker against the room and reflect through the window space. He hesitated a moment to consider his next actions, then moved on forward.

During the time Zer had started upon his path making his way to Julian's, Darla had returned from her investigation and had begun to settle in for the evening. It was amazing they hadn't both bumped into one another. Their timing was so close, but the direction of approach slightly different. She had gone around the perimeter of the village and traversed the disheveled Festival grounds. Some villagers were preparing stands and tidying up. Everyone was cheerful and pleasant, saying hello as she passed. The grass was a magnificent rich emerald hue, and the flowers and shrubbery were in full trimmed bloom. The scene resembled an old masterpiece in its tranquillity and color. Truly it was a miracle that such beauty had been left unspoiled by the Gotts. Thank goodness they had never made it this far south! She continued, and along the way came upon two herbalists she was meant to have met before all the trouble had so delayed her. They were working on their stands when one noticed Darla and excitedly called out:

"D! D! Is that you? Where have you been? We thought you were...Er...I don't know what we thought, but it is so good to see you. How..."

"Hello. What a surprise to come across you two! I got mixed up and caught in the trouble," she indicated northward, "Had to take to hiding. It was close, but it will be a long story for another night," she wanted to avoid talking about herself, and so turned the conversation to them. "How are things here with you?"

They spoke for a short while, and then 'D' bade them: "Good eve, my friends. Tomorrow we will sip a tankard and I will tell my story," she knew full well that by then she and the nephews would be long departed upon their journey, but she didn't want anyone to know these plans. During these strange times she wasn't certain whom the *Evil* could possess or use to discover the whereabouts of the *thieves* of the Key. 'D' didn't believe in coincidences and regarded this abrupt encounter with, what some might view to be, paranoia. The *Evil* would sink to any type of subterfuge in order to find success!

"Only sip! No, we will make a long night of it and catch up," said one.

"Yes. That would be most welcome!" added the other.

'D' nodded, shook both of their arms, and turned away. The two friends smiled at each other, pleased to know that their friend was safe. They continued waving after Darla until she had advanced and disappeared on the path toward Julian's.

She quickly arrived at the cottage, her mind on the alert for the slightest questionable item. She was fatigued. Hopefully Eruinn and Thiunn would be back by now, and then the three could prepare for the morning trip.

Upon arriving at the cottage, she saw that they weren't there yet! She entered, found her way further inside, and waited in the room with the fireplace. She began a nervous pacing. She wondered on the dangers that lay ahead. As it was getting dark, she lit a fire and a Beezel wax candle. There was still no sign of Eruinn or Thiunn. She sat on the big smooth green leather chair and felt like a monarch on a throne, it was so very large. Facing the stone fireplace, her mind drifted to the father of the son who had built this hearth. It had been so long since she had seen Julian's father. It had been so long since his passing, and yet now for the first time since knowing both, she missed the son more. *'Where was Julian? Was he safe?'* She directed her thought to the warmth. There came no answer. The fireplace remained stoic. Her eyes caressed the hard stone, looking for the craft mark of the Stoneman. Darla knew where to find it. There to the right of the hearth: a chisel, a hammer, a shield of old and a key—and a KEY! She jumped up and closely examined the stones. *Could there be something more here?*

It was at the moment of her noticing of the 'mark' that Zer, who was just outside the cottage, decided to wait no longer. He moved to the front doorway and carefully asked:

"Hello? Anyone there?" he continued to enter the cottage and move down the main hallway which led to the fireplace room.

A startled Darla turned in the direction of the asking. She heard the voice, muffled by determined weighty footsteps, coming her way! 'The Gotts?' was her first consideration. She hastily looked for a hiding space and in doing so placed her hand upon the hearthstone with the Stonemans' markings. In a desperate yearning she called out in her thoughts to Julian for an answer. Suddenly came a response, but Darla was not aware of it. She squeezed herself into the shadow of the corner gap on the right side of the solid stone hearth, and waited. She felt at the very least she would be able to lunge out at the intruder and cause a surprise. She waited as the footstep drew closer. *'The candle!'* She realized that in the rush she had forgotten and it had been left alight! She quickly tried unsuccessfully, to blow it out from her present position, but it was clear that there was no time, and soon stopped, for whoever approached, was almost there.

"Hello? Anyone here?...Strange?" Zer was just finishing his walk down the hallway and about to enter the room where both Darla and the lit candle stood. He noticed the silence and could feel the tension in the air. Upon entering the room he noticed the candle and its light, which flickered more with his new motion, filling the area: the fire was also alive.

"Whoever is here come on out. I will not harm you. There is nothing to fear. Come out." But there was no movement. Zer began looking around the room, his examining glance flowed throughout. There was nothing. He moved around the room; stepped forward and stopped. He looked right into Darla's face. Darla froze, considering the next action. Then:

"Whoever is here please come out! There will be no harm." He stood and appeared to be staring into her. But he wasn't. Zer could only see the dimly lit stone fireplace edge, its mantle and the joining of it forming an empty corner to the wall of the cottage. There was a window about an arms length away, which peeked onto the back garden and the undergrowth beyond. He felt as if he was close to something. He almost could smell the sweet sweat of something. It felt as though he was being watched, just like before, but more intense. There was a hint of a panting breath.

Darla's thoughts raced and questioned: *"He's looking right at me! What is going on?!"*

Zer turned away and walked back to the hallway. Before he entered he extinguished the flame, and spoke out loud to himself: "Well, whoever it was they sure left in a hurry! Probably transients. I'll put extra patrols into the area tomorrow." He took one last inspection and left.

Darla was bedazzled! He hadn't seen her, but he had looked directly into her eyes! She checked to make certain that she could see herself, by raising a hand in front of her. There it was. No problem! What had happened? She heard the intruder leave the cottage and go down the pathway into the night.

"Very odd!? Why didn't he see me? Who was that?" She had stumbled onto some magic in this cottage, but could not begin to explain or understand the process that had activated the power, but she was grateful it existed!

She stepped out of her crunched hiding place and, after a moment more of wondering at its triggering, speculated as to whether Julian knew of this method of hiding within the openness of his home. She shuffled in the direction of the candle and finding the light she had earlier used, lit it again. She returned to sitting down on the couch before the fireplace quietly waiting till Eruinn and Thiunn arrived. Her mind remained on the image of the intruder. He had the resemblance of an official. Perhaps a member of the local patrol. As these pictures continued in her busy head, without noticing, she fell asleep. It was long overdue and well deserved. Soon it would be morning.

- - - - - - - - - - - - - - - - - -

It did not take very long. Eruinn and Thiunn found their way home without hindrance. They both hurried up to their small home, calling out when they were close enough for their mother to hear:

"Mother! Mother! We're home!" But silence was their only answer. They called again as they came closer, but still no stirring. They became frightened. *Where was Mother?*

- - - - - - - - - - - - - - - - - -

While these three had been making their discoveries on the way to and in Jard, other eyes that had been searching the area of the South and were honing in on their newly activated connection within the Magic. It was the *Evil*, Dorluc. He was using his view screen to seek out the thieves and any traces of the Key and *Passwords*. There had been a tiny depletion in the Magic, like that at the castle with Merm, in the area of Jard. He was grabbing at anything that might help him to find the Key! As a result, Dorluc had arranged with one of his ethereal allies, to rummage through the cottage in Jard; the one that had been first discovered and reported by Flal and Logue as the starting place of the thieves. Perhaps there would be something that could lead them. Till now, they were uncertain as to whom or where to follow.

Dorluc was aggravated and in a foul temper. It was taking far too long to discover the whereabouts of the

The Cottage of Lenore

thieves of the Key. He reset the view screen several times giving it a smaller search area in an attempt to speed up the process. He was prepared to keep searching, nothing was expected to result.

The view screen was very old. It had been created by the Old Ones and sent to this place along with Dorluc and his followers. It was meant to torment these prisoners and remind them of the price of their treachery! Dorluc quickly discovered its greater value—to watch and listen to any in the corporal worlds, not to be seen! Much information could be gathered and used, along with the *Evil*, to great advantage. In the past, once Dorluc was prepared to re-establish his corporal existence, it had helped him to monitor and influence Lord Ho, but something had gone wrong and Ho was destroyed by other powers before Dorluc could escape! Dorluc did not want the same type of disappointment this time with Merm.

Dorluc was upset with the recent difficulties and changes within the Balance. He must deal with these intruders before they upset his plans of escape by alerting 'others' who may also be dormant and waiting to be triggered. The longer it took to find them, the greater the chances of things going wrong. It was very timely when both these two young ones and the female materialized. Finally he had located the three from Norkleau! He felt reassured in his prowess and abilities. He privately congratulated himself for trusting in the view screen, though he had always had his doubts, *he knew that the view screen would locate them.* Not many had the power of the Old Ones and he was pleased to find them again after the subterranean passages in Norkleau! To be lured so simply into the cottage made Dorluc realize that the first young 'Chosen One' was obviously a novice, and the second, weak in magic of 'knowing' or 'seeing'.

The female had brought attention to her by a foolish use of the Magic, by accessing it to go into hiding at the cottage. That was something he would never have done! It was unfathomable! Perhaps they were not aware of his presence! That could explain this sloppiness! Once the trickle of the Magic was noticed, the view screen immediately sought after the source! Now all those attuned to the shift within the Balance were alerted. Dorluc and his congregation had been watching everything since those moments, thrilled and smug in their self praise. It would be easy planning their next actions against these three! They were like lost young. Dorluc would snare them and regain the Key once he could determine which of the three possessed it. He spoke to his group as they scrutinized the scenes being displayed:

"The Old Ones will regret this mistake of sending 'these' to challenge my greatness! I will cause a tremendous shifting of the Magic and catch each of these 'Chosen Ones'. They will suffer unlike any before. They are no match for Dorluc! We must use every soul to serve our purpose," he stood over the large illuminated slab, crossed his arms and placed a spindly finger against a ragged dry old lip, "this female with the sword of the Old will be first to fall she will be ...a sensuous 'toy' to awaken and be entertained, after my return from this place." He held out his arms indicating the room and extending to the land of no form to which he and his followers were exiled.

This event had elevated Dorluc's mood. He sensed a control being restored over the situation of the stolen Key. It had never been so close and he was not going to miss a second time! He still required the physical assistance of the real worlds to obtain the complete Magic of Old. His power right now, though threatening, could only influence. Someone else had to 'unlock' him along with the *Passwords*.

"Master...the Magic is stronger with the female. Maybe she holds the Key? The two young ones show only a weak power. We need to get hold of them. Nothing is revealed through the viewer," one of his gathering was commenting on the pictures being presented, "How can we accomplish this now that the Gotts have been beaten?"

Dorluc fell silent with thought. Then:

"We have no more need of the Gott Troops. We can use other means now that the Worlds are safe," he had a grin as he said the words, "there will be less chance of further interruption of our purpose. Only these three can stand in our way. We must enliven the *moles* that dwell in the worlds. They will be of assistance in reclaiming that which is rightfully mine! With the festivities there must be some nearby. You will seek them out and say the necessary words. They must not cause harm to the female or young ones until the Key is restored to us. Now get to your tasks, and let no-one fail me!" Dorluc's last sentence rang through the room. To fail would mean their exclusion from release with Dorluc. Not one of them would allow that outcome. They would succeed, not for Dorluc, but for their own carnification.

When they had all left, Dorluc remained alone facing the slab. Slowly it turned from viewing to a glowing misty blue gray form. The form was very old and not distinguishable. A voice emanated:

"You have news?" The sound came from the direction of the form and was clearly more powerful and older than Dorluc.

"Yes Old One. All that you told is coming true. I have found the three," Dorluc was fearfully reporting.

"And what of the Stoneman?"

"There are two young ones, but they are newly ordained, and a female. There is not another."

"There is another!" the image was not pleased with Dorluc's indiscreetness, "he must be found before it is too late. It is the Keeper they seek. They must not find the *Keeper*!"

"But where..." Dorluc was groveling.

"Find them all before we next meet. I will not again display my power before them...If you fail..." the image faded but the words echoed out.

Dorluc was perplexed. He couldn't understand what kept interfering with his magic, causing him delays and mishaps. Far too much was at stake!

Chapter 2.

On and on he traversed through the Burning Forest. His legs felt like they might at any moment give way under the strain of the past few hours. He sighed as he continued the effort of the walk, sensing his paranoia of the immediate environment. It was just dusk. Straggly looking *daru wood* with the dark gray bark and spindly green needles of coniferous genera surrounded him. These were the Moonfruit trees. The forests of the ancient times; the days of the Magic of the Old Ones. All this brought back the childhood tales and folklore, which amazingly were still vivid in his memory.

He walked, keeping a weary eye out for the green mossy rocks which occasionally forced him to zigzag his path. He had not yet stopped for rest, food or drink; partially because of the fear of his pursuit by the *Evil* of Dorluc and the Lord Merm, and partially due to the lack of any provisions. How he missed the company and security of Darla and his nephews. He knew somehow that they were well and that they too, would soon rejoin him and complete the journey they had all started together from his tiny village of Jard. Jard, how lovely and peaceful his thoughts became, but it was a home which was lying farther and farther to the south with each tired step forward. His mind was jarred back to the present, as he stumbled over a half hidden moss covered boulder. *Where was he meant to go?* He knew that this northwesterly direction was correct, but as to the final destination, or how far away he must travel—this knowledge eluded him.

The forest was darker now. A mixture of rocks and

trees. The ground under his path was undulating. There was a strange freshness to the air and a feeling of a greatness, or a lurking power, nearby. He felt as though eyes were upon him, watching each movement, sensing both the fear and exhilaration within his tired person. He dared not stop, but his weariness would soon overtake him, and he would then collapse. Julian knew this wasn't wise in such a dark treed mysterious place, especially since he could only see through the first two or three lines of trees from his path. Who knew what lay waiting out there, amidst the many thin trunks, boulders, and the damp torridness of the woods. This wasn't pleasant, he had never liked camping, or its inconveniences!

"Ohhh," he blurted out. "What a cold mess this has all become!"

He shuddered and pulled his browny gray burlap cloak tighter together in an attempt to ward off the beginning outdoor chill. The sounds of the night creatures who inhabited this space were slowly growing in number. There was the sudden snap of a broken twig off in the distance. The noise of insects, and the cry of—something, Julian wasn't sure he wanted to know! It was imperative that he find a safe haven to rest through the night. The fear of the Burning Forest was now taking priority over the danger of his pursuers!

As a child he had been told the stories of the Burning Forest; the fact that the never ending fires, which spred from part to part, were set by strange beings to keep out wanderers. These beings lived secretly in the Forest, away from the other worlds. No-one had ever proven their existence, though the stories recounted numerous encounters. They were portrayed as mischievous and unfriendly. Julian, as a youngster, had always enjoyed the tales of them that his father would laboriously tell. He became fascinated more than afraid, as if he knew that these tales were not really true, though he wasn't completely certain. It was the way his father had told the stories that made Julian develop affinity towards these Forest Dwellers. He always thought, and it was still the case now as he wandered through 'their' lands, that one day he would discover the truth behind the tales and folklore.—He would find these beings! But that was just the adventurous bravado of a young one living in the secure life of Jard, or so he believed! So much had changed in the last while that he was not able to separate truth, myth or reality with any confidence! He felt that he was about to stumble right into a story out of his childhood. *Was this all a dream?* Would he awaken to find himself in his warm bed, in his safe home, in Jard; with the smell of breakfast being prepared and his father calling out to him to: *'Get up!'* The fatigue was clearly taking its toll upon his mind as well as his body. He must find a place to rest, and the Moonfruit trees were the only available answer. The ground was too cold and unprotected. The rocks and boulders already home to many unknown things. High up and cradled in the boughs of these ancient trees was his only hope of safety and undisturbed rest.

He stopped in mid step at the rising end of his path. As far as he could see there was not any tree or spot that encouraged this necessitated interruption of his flight. Continuing to reconnoiter, his eyes were drawn to one lone and grand Pine, standing on higher ground. Its main trunk was much wider than the other nearby trees, and its branches appeared mightier, visually reminiscent of a Patriarch domineering over a family of other lesser, and obviously younger bark. These were just feelings, or instincts that ran through Julian. He trusted 'that' spot more than all the others within his viewpoint. He trusted *that* tree. It was drawing him with the familiarity of a dear close friend. Without consciously noticing all of these thoughts and realizations, Julian continued his step and made directly for the old Moonfruit.

As he approached, Julian felt as though voices had replaced the eyes that he had earlier felt upon him, voices that were beckoning, calling out to him to: *'Come....come old friend, it is safe. It has been long since we last...'* When he arrived at the grand old Moonfruit tree he quickly and cautiously surveyed the immediate area. He walked slowly around the large trunk; feeling satisfied about the safety of the place, he turned his view upward, hoping to find a level in the tree to which he could tie a few loose sticks and make a bed. Not more than five lengths up there was a suitable joining of two sturdy looking branches.

After collecting a dozen large sticks of about an arm's length each and ripping out some long strands of the sweet grass that grew near the side of his pathway, Julian attempted to climb the tree. It was an awkward looking sight! Sweet grass tucked in his shirt and sticks pushed in between his trousers and his belt. At the start he jumped a few times trying to catch hold of the first branch. Finally it seemed as if the branch lowered, allowing him to hold on and be lifted off the ground. Julian rationalized that it must have been his tired imagination. Then upward and another branch or so and he reached his goal. Satisfied with his lofty position, he was now ready to make his bed and sleep.

There was a lovely breeze in the trees. The sound was a *whissshing* as it meandered through the dizzy heights of his bunk. Julian felt a oneness with the forest. Feeling relaxed and protected for the first time since his bed in Jard, he lay upon the mattress of wood and was lulled to a deep sleep by the cutting sound of the wind, and the gentle motion of the branches. As Julian's weary body and soul drifted he was not aware of the shrill melody and lightly sweetened air that also began to drift through the tree tops. From tree to tree it flowed. Soothing and peaceful.

The Moonfruit trees were communing, the breeze carrying their sense much like a Beezel pollinating as it flew from flower to flower. The Moonfruit could not really move, but they did bend. The Moonfruit did not speak, yet they did talk. Their way was empathic.

There was a great deal of magic in their fruit and its ability to affect the mind of the unsuspecting wanderer in this great forest. They held old wisdom within their rippled gray bark. They were protectors and messengers, passing on their observances to the Forest Dwellers who lived in their midst, but deeper within the dark of the Burning Forest.

- - - - - - - - - - - - - - - - - -

Alert to the entry of this lone traveler had begun early, as Julian had entered the forest. While he traveled, the Moonfruit had been reporting to the 'Dwellers', and awaiting a response. It was their task to tire the traveler, to slow him down until a clear directive was sensed from the Dwellers. This had not been a very difficult task in this particular instance, since Julian was already exhausted from his trip and ordeal at Norkleau. It had been easy to sense the fear in Julian but there was also a strange familiarity, one that was very old, belonging to the earlier times. The grand old Moonfruit remembered such a familiarity from before, but it was with a different traveler. It had been a very long time ago.

Some parts of the folklore and tales of the Forest were true. Wanderers were generally not welcome and were treated with suspicion; even though most traveling through or near the Forest were never consciously aware of who was menacing, or what was happening to them. A haunting fear possessed their minds, which quickly forced them back out and away. This was an effective method of deterrence, as no one could physically place blame on anyone else other than the *magic of the woods*. The 'word of mouth' would expand as each recounting of every known experience of the Forest, progressed and found its way from world to world.

Most parts of the stories were not accurate. The fires to be found nearer the northeast sections of the

Forest were not, as had been told, set on purpose. They were instead the natural hazards of nature, and it had been impossible to extinguish their flame with any continued success. Control was all that could be expected; a control that was more a result of luck and the normal balance of weather, than any other decided effort! The Dwellers attempted to create ditches to stop or at least change the arbitrary direction of the flames that both wind and spark would choose. They were unable to have tremendous influence using their meager tools and numbers. For now, there still existed a geographic barrier of hills, rocks and more importantly the Marshlands of the Pass river, which had so far been most effective; a condition to which the Moonfruit trees in the southern tip of the Forest were grateful! The threat, however historically rare, remained in memory, for under the right conditions anything was possible. Recently there was a renewed concern that perhaps the right conditions were near!

Great faith was placed in the Dwellers to watch over all. 'They' of the Burning Forest were a small tribe, living in harmony with 'their' home. Primitive would best describe their outward appearance, but the Dwellers were really a highly developed community, working and living together for their common good.

At one time in the distance of memory, each Dweller had been a member of other villages and communities of the worlds, till the jealousies or insecurities of others had made them outcasts. Individually, Dwellers were free thinking and sophisticated in vision. They thought their questioning and frankness a necessity in order to maintain an open, tolerant, free and durable community. Unfortunately, their philosophies and presence scrutinized too efficiently the fiber of their respective villages and went beyond the abilities of those communities capacity to understand. These few thinkers were far too advanced and soon represented a threat to the average villager who was only concerned with the daily struggle of basic existence and frightened by the motivation and agenda of those free thinkers. Eventually the incongruencies and the self interest; the lack of understanding or willingness to perfect, preserve or respect (though this was never openly admitted) of the main stream members of these communities, was venomous in its underhanded attempts to silence those questioning. Intolerance was swift.

As a result, this small community far away and in the Forest had developed. Its ancestors came together to form a uniquely open yet reclusive environment in which the members could live. Each member of the Dwellers cut their ties with the non Forest worlds and set upon a path of learning and living in harmony and tolerance, a path which had made them guardians of nature.

Out of the Forest, the Dwellers had secretly carved an existence that would endure long after the destruction of the other non understanding worlds. But that had been so long ago and now most outside knowledge of them that existed, was accepted only as myth. They were left alone, unbothered, until now. There had been changes felt. There had been a darkness, and then it was gone! Something had disturbed the Balance of Old. It would be their duty to redirect it. This was the agreement made by them long ago with the Old Ones.

The Dwellers, unlike other guardians, were always aware of their responsibilities to the worlds and the Balance. In the earlier years they had quite unintentionally, from their point of reference, encountered the majestic castle upon which Norkleau now rested. They were awed by the achievements and considerateness for nature, of the ones found in the *City that sparkled*, for that was how they referred to it. The Old Ones realized upon this meeting, that they were dealing with individuals very similar to themselves in philosophy, but not power, who needed a safe community. They arranged an understanding, with their neighbors of the Forest, to shield them against the *Evil*, from whatever source, that most assuredly would continue to seek and eliminate them further.

During those ancient years much had been learned, and the sturdy small community of Forest Dwellers had thrived. It was only after the Old Ones 'went on' that they, just like the 'age', went into a decline, a dormancy in terms of the other worlds. The existence of these forest creatures eventually became entwined and a part of the folklore of the Old Ones.

Due to these myths and their location, the Dwellers had been forgotten and left alone. Even the Gotts,— even Lord Ho, who was too focused on the Balance and power of the Key, relegated these legends in his thoughts to meaningless superstition. As a result, the Separation Wars had never scathed them. Later, Lord Merm ignored them much like Ho, and Dorluc never considered their ancient friendships when making his plans. This was about to be modified. Not as a conscious effort, but rather as a result of Julian's flight and purpose. Others followed after him to recapture what, in their mind was theirs. In the process they would discover the secrets of the Burning Forest.

The Dwellers would be placed in an awkward situation, and duty bound to not stand silently by, but to act. This would risk their continued anonymity. A risk that some in their number did not wish to take. It was not out of fear that some would initially disagree, rather a long accepted and in-bred isolationism. After all, as far as the other non Forest worlds were concerned, they were not real anyway! Why should time be spent helping the descendants of those who had turned their own ancestors away!?

In the security of the ages some Dwellers had forgotten the dangers that remained in the other worlds. Dangers of the type the Old Ones had warned about and given powers to help ward off in times of need. The powers had never been used; or had they? How was it that the secrecy of the Dwellers had been upheld? Had not the cooperation and awareness of the Moonfruit been accomplished? Yes, the power had been used, at least a little.

With the Old Ones gone, the Dwellers would have to reveal themselves if the threat, as suggested by the changes, became real! Their power was not one of violent destruction, instead, it was the power of thought, thought through persuasion and alteration. Form could be transposed, and thoughts adjusted. In the past this was felt to be strong enough in conjunction with the Old Ones' Magic, but now with the absence of the Ones of the *City that sparkled,* a concern to the potentialities and threats arose amongst the tribe. These concerns would have to be addressed and decisions quickly made by those who led the inner forest world.

Leadership of the tribe was by a group of elders. The 'Elders' of the tribe had always kept track of the outside by means of visions and dream travel. The power of dream enabled them to see and hear without ever leaving the safety of their forest home. By this means an accurate accounting could be made to the rest of the tribe, keeping all abreast and alerted to developments beyond the Burning Forest. It was necessary to know the level of knowledge of outsiders, to the awareness of their forest community. This procedure had been easy enough in the past, but lately there had been many newer disturbing elements, such as the uncovering of the Key and the *Passwords of Promise.* The Dwellers were aware of the existence of these items, for the Old Ones had confided in them, asking in return their promise to provide immunity and passage to anyone in possession of these. They were sworn to help any who possessed the magic of the words. This oath had never needed to be used. Now, with the events of the outside and the entry of this weary traveler, who the Moonfruit had just reported and remarked how they believed they were able to commune, it seemed that the Dwellers' long outstanding obligations to the Old Ones would soon begin to be called upon. It was an opportunity, according to the Elders, to repay old debts of friendship. A 'convening' of the tribe was quickly called.

- - - - - - - - - - - - - - - - - -

The Moonfruit were still awaiting the response from deep within the woods. It would come, from one element of the woods to the other, passed on till eventually it was 'sensed' by all the Pine in the south of the Forest. What was taking so long? Usually answers were quickly given. Half the night had gone without 'sense'! The traveler was deep in sleep, but that couldn't last forever.

As they waited, the trees caressed Julian, continuing the repose. They created peace within his mind. Strangely, this traveler seemed to have the power of 'sensing', something that intrigued the grand Moonfruit and pushed it to investigate more. It stretched its branches, like antennae and focused its 'sensing' upon Julian. In waves it probed and stroked the sleeping awareness of him. As it probed it sent assurances of peace and friendship. Oddly, the Moonfruit felt as if Julian understood, but no answer was returned. It continued.

"Stop your search. Leave this one alone. He is a Keeper."

This sudden voicing of 'sense' caused a startling not only to the grand Moonfruit, but also the other Pine, who all shared in the probing of sense by their tap root, *Fon*. Fon only once before had encountered a traveler, not of the wood, who could commune, but never had it *heard* this voice. Moonfruit only sensed!

"Stop Fon. I am the one from before. This is my son. He carries the hope of our worlds, the Balance of the Three. He must remain unharmed. The *Evil* even now pursues."

Fon was even more surprised. How did this voicing

know its name? Waves went through the Pine. After some moments, Fon searched its thought for a clearer identification of the one from before. Finally it located the time. It was not possible for this traveler to be the son. The once before was during the age of the Old Ones!

"That is not so. This one is too young, and the other long ago," Fon replied in sense.

"Yes. You begin to recall. I am the first. This is my seed, my son of my son of my...we are the same yet different. But we are not young. We carry the Magic of the Old Ones, of Dali, of Lorn...do you remember the thoughts?"

"Yes. How shall we know you are the one? Long ages have past and we are at wonder upon your return. How shall we be certain of what is said?"

"How many *voicings* have you of the south Forest heard? Is it not your way to sense? *Tell me,* how do you explain this unusual occurrence?"

"It is difficult to have thoughts on this, it has never happened in our age. Who are your masters?"

The interchange of words was telepathic and continued. Fon was cautious not only as a result of its nature, but also as a result of the sensing of the changes in the other worlds which were as yet unexplained and approaching. Was this a voice of the Old times or a trick for some, as yet, unknown purpose? Who was this traveler of such importance? What did he carry? Why had not the Dwellers intervened? The Moonfruit were steady and not easily dissuaded by strangeness. Confirmation was required.

The mentioning of Dali and Lorn was extraordinary. Only the oldest Pine could have sense of these times. It was due to these ancients that the Dwellers had been safeguarded and the Moonfruit preserved. Dali had saved the wood from the destruction of the axesaw. It was in those innocent times when the Moonfruit were open and welcoming to all outsiders, unaware of the danger or the greed of the cutters of wood to make profit and not respect their natural ways, that they had been almost decimated by the axesaw. So unprepared were they in those times. It hurt to think how they had to change in order to survive. The trusting was lost, replaced by wariness and bitterness.

Lorn had helped to re-graft the forest, but most of the longest standing bark had perished in the cutting, and was beyond replanting. He spent many sunrises nurturing and tending till eventually their roots increased in number. Over the ages it had never returned to the same level of wood. Mostly young grew. It needed a long time. Even now most of the wood was not more than two hundred rings! Many more layers of bark were necessary in order to reach the wisdom of the before times. Fon alone stood, with a branch of others scattered throughout the south Forest, to lead, teach and raise. The mention of these two, had displayed great knowledge of the past. It was a temptation to accept the voice, but that was not the way of the Moonfruit.

"I have no masters, but am part of them. Come...it is the moment of asking. From deep behind, reap the benefit and sow the bark of rings." The voice spoke again.

This was the oldest of secret greetings, only the communed knew its sensing. It could still be trickery. The caution of Fon remained.

The bark of rings was the story of the life of a wood. As each moment scurried on, the trunk thickened. With each new layer of an age came the rings. They were embedded within the trunk, full of the knowledge and ways of Pine. To use it as greeting demanded complete ability and opening in the art of 'sensing'. It was an imprinting, a request of communion between the greeted wood. Whatever this voice was, it knew the ways of the Forest! No outsider could ever have acquired such skills. Fon if not fully convinced, decided to accept the words of voicing—for now!

"You have great knowledge of us. We acknowledge

its depth. We will stop our probing. What do you ask beyond?"

Fon had sensed and in a flash made the response. Before its next voicing, the other one answered:

"I have had many names. All were me and all were not. I am my son and my father. I am a Stoneman. A master of trade, and servant to all."

Fon suddenly sensed the greater meaning. A *Stoneman*! Those were the agents of the Old Ones. The Keepers of the Balance, and protectors of the wisdom of the *City that sparkled*. It was now finally beginning to make 'sense'!

Chapter 3.

All were gathered for the convening. Every Dweller was expected to attend. The group of seven Elders would sit in the lowest point of the 'place of convening'.

The 'place of convening' was situated in a dry 'V' river valley. It had tenanted a small tributary that meandered its way through the Forest until it eventually flowed into the Marshlands of the Pass river. Water no longer moistened the banks, which were very sloped and treed with the narrow tall trunks of new wood.

This was the place where the Dwellers met, discussed, and decided on those important matters which affected and therefore required the general consensus of the gathered tribe. All Dwellers had the right to make a clear choice and have questions addressed. It was the way of long ago, established and meticulously followed throughout the generations.

The light from the moon permeated the numerous thin trees with their slender finger branches, spotlighting an area that was circular and devoid of vegetation. Here was the political arena; if the Dwellers could be said to have one, which resembled an outdoor theater. The area had, before the bed was dry, been a large circular pool where the water of the river gathered, before it picked up enough quantity and continued to flow. Now only pebbles and stones gathered amongst the dried leaves and dead rotting twigs. One lone log was lying upon the ground, providing space for the members of the tribe to sit. Or if they preferred, some could go higher up, reclining on the steep banks to either side, and watch as life's performance progressed. Most of the surrounding area displayed the clear evidence of the frequent trampling by the Dwellers. This was their center meeting place; private and hidden.

Unlike their politics, there was no center of habitation. The Dwellers preferred to scatter themselves throughout the vicinity, within voice of one another. A few lived under the ground in leaf covered cave-like mud houses; little chimneys rose through the leaf thatched roofs allowing the almost undetectable smoke to rise out of their abode. The majority however, took to the trees, they tended to build nest-like homes that, like the terrene, blended and were naturally camouflaged within their environment. Vines provided access to the heights. In either situation, the Dwellers lived well.

Their appearance reflected the life of the woods. They appeared unkempt, but they were not dirty. Their eyes were fiery and alive. There was a childlike quality to their actions and responses with each other while they relaxed, but a determined and very old self-assuredness exuded them when they were engaged in more serious events, such as the one that was about to commence. Their dress was 'of the Forest' and their speech was light and jovial. As they gathered, they slowly greeted and chatted amongst each other, making themselves comfortable in the spot where they usually sat upon the slope or bank. They were a mixture of tall and short, male and female. They were individuals yet at the same time communal.

"Members of the tribe. Please pay heed," came the official call.

They all fell silent as the Elders took places on the river bed dais. One bearded Elder spoke:

"For long times we have watched the outsiders and their change. Never before has there been such concern. Now there is danger of great changings. A traveler brings the *Evil* of the other worlds upon us. We have seen this in our watch. There will be no turning back this traveler. He is of the Old of the city of sparkle. He is not our destroyer but from them he is in flight. He is the one, like before. They follow, and they seek the power of the Balance of Three. He carries the hope and brings the great fear. We now must repay the debt of before. Darkness has not yet gone from the forest." The oratory did not flow smoothly, but evoked a communication that was based upon both word and the rhythm poetic scarcity.

There was a moment of silence as the Elder stood waiting. It was the way. The questioning could begin:

"Why is this traveler here? What force brings him and should it not help him pass? How can we deliver this one?"

The Elder surveyed the tribe, seeking a response. A tall young Dweller stood, and facing the questioner, replied:

"The Moonfruit have sensed the traveler. This very night he lies in their branches. They say he communes."

There was a sound of astonishment.

"…He reminds them of once before. Their influence will not stop his purpose." Again a pause of silence followed in which there were mumblings, but no more direct debate.

The Elder spoke:

"It is time. We must gather and help this one on his journey. He must be helped. We will bring him to us, to discover the need."

There was again the sound of shock rippling through the membership. No one had ever been shown the way to their home!

"Why do we act so?" spoke the first questioner.

The Elder thought, then answered:

"We have seen this one in our dream. He is of great company. His tribe old. He is hard as the Stone, but flies and touches the sparkle."

The Dwellers language was deeply entangled with their lore. Not many words were needed to express the prophesies or their meanings. The Old Ones had provided and the Dwellers agreed. There were signs given to identify the need. The first ones were now being revealed: The reference to: *'traveler who would commune,'* *'A darkness approaching the Forest,'* *'The stone and the sparkle.'* These were all the signs of the One who carried the power of the words.

The gathered Dwellers all silently appreciated the meanings. It was just difficult to believe that the lore was indeed coming into reality!

The Elder stood awhile longer and waited. There was no more comment. As was their custom, the last words spoken and not questioned again, remained. They had made the choice. Even though the full ramifications were unknown, they each understood the powerful magic involved in this choosing, and that their part in aiding it was necessary. Two of their most capable members would now be sent to bring them the traveler. This was the way. *Two would arrive*, as the lore had told, *just before he fell from the Moonfruit and into the Evil grasp!*

- - - - - - - - - - - - - - - - -

Response to the reporting of the Moonfruit finally made its way to the southeastern entrance of the Burning Forest. The timing was oracular. It came just a few moments after the thought voicing had stopped speaking with Fon and just as Fon stopped its sensing of Julian. The message flowed with the wind over the branch tops of the Pine. They were being asked: *'Do not disturb the traveler, but allow him to rest until the arrival of Quei and Thodox, who are en route.'* Before their arrival, it was suggested that the Moonfruit: *'increase their sensing and inform the Dwellers immediately of any changes or of any other travelers approaching the Forest.'* Fon quickly organized the wood toward the task, not allowing time for the other bark to consider the recent peculiarities.

Quei and Thodox would not take long to arrive.

During all of these events Julian had remained asleep. It was well deserved. His mind and body drifted into a total rejuvenating rest. This was the *dream state*, where those with power could speak with each another, past and future. Since Norkleau and the visit of the image of his father, Julian without comprehension, was able to reach this level. Tonight it happened again.

"Julian. Julian," came the same voice of the Norkleau passages.

A picture of he and his father standing in a dark empty place formed slowly in his dream.

"Father. Again? What's happening? I don't..."

The image cut in.

"You must go to the Dwellers. They have the knowledge you need to complete your task. On the other side stands the destination. They know the path, but not the location. The Three must together be placed. The *Evil* one is close. Do not waste an instant."

Julian noticed the half rhyme of the words. It was as if deeper hidden meaning stood between each phrase. What Julian did not know was the intent of 'his father' to influence and encourage his own abilities to make the proper decisions, but not to actualize them on his behalf. That would be misuse of the Magic and only help the *Evil* of Dorluc.

The mention of the Three, brought Julian's dreaming attention to thoughts of Darla, Eruinn and Thiunn. Had they all survived Norkleau? The 'leaving' had been so sudden and unannounced! He felt guilty for this abandonment of his companions. If there had been another choice...no...the *Evil* was drawn to their collective energy, like a beacon the new rift in the Magic was notifying and locating them. Separated, this beam would diffuse, there would be no one clear direction for the *Evil* to track. In the uncertainty, valuable time could be gained and so Julian was able to flee relatively unnoticed! He wasn't certain as to how he knew all of this, but he hoped this head start could give him a long enough lead!

His father's voice paused for a short time. Julian was still deep in the dream state. All of these thoughts were being placed by the others within him. There was a newer urgency to them. Many half completed thoughts passed before his sleeping consciousness. His dreaming mind began to wonder at the nearness of his *evil* pursuers. He noticed a presence. It was difficult to identify, but there was a definite 'probing'. This alarm commenced the process to awaken him from the depth of the sleep. He must not allow, due to the luxury of his rest, the gap between them to close any more than necessary!

- - - - - - - - - - - - - - - -

Quei and Thodox were anxious to cover the distance to the Moonfruit rapidly. The Elders had spoken briefly with each privately, then bade them away. They were to take the harder most direct paths. It had been very tiring, but the importance of their charge invigorated and pushed them on even faster!

Quei was outspoken and had questioned the Elders at the convening. He was strongly supportive of the membership, but felt a responsibility to always question when, in his opinion, others became complacent.

He was strong and amongst the very best of followers. There wasn't a thing in the forest he couldn't find. Even the smallest marking caught his tuned eye. Extremely methodical and respected, he never aspired to become an Elder. A rugged handsome individualist, he would easily have received support, but preferred to remain in his mild and happy life, having little need for the added concerns of that office. He loved freedom.

Thodox was the dreamer, and like Quei, thoroughly skilled in the arts of the forest. He was an expert hunter, and the most loyal of companions. Not as out-spoken as Quei, but his listening ear carefully weighed all that occurred; his judgment of circumstances never far off the mark. Honor was placed foremost and himself second. He was the romantic traditionalist, seeing life through an innocent idealism. This did not imply he was of weak nature nor undecided, but whenever he could choose, he would savor the ritualistic process, rather than the utilitarian completion of task. He understood both sides.

Through the forest they ran. First it was through the well trodden paths that lead toward the southeastern entrance. Then as the trails curved, both agreed to step off and make their own passage. In the dark it was difficult to anticipate the hazards, but eventually they had come most of the way. They now had stopped momentarily to refresh themselves.

"Do you imagine this traveler to be a threat?" Quei was contemplating what tactics should be exercised in making contact with this unknown outsider. He had never met an outsider this close before, and wasn't certain at what might be the outcome.

"The poor soul is probably scared to death! Any outsider who would stay the night after entering the wood of the Moonfruit, must be running from something pretty awful. I hope we don't meet it while we are introducing ourselves!" Thodox was trying to lighten the mood.

"Perhaps. But what if this traveler takes us for his adversary," the idea was left hanging, "We should consider our approach. Just in case?" Quei was asking for an opinion more than making a statement.

"It wouldn't hurt to be cautious, but let's not expect the worst. If we're lucky he'll still be asleep. Then we <u>all</u> could be better prepared for the deliverance and help reduce the jolt of first meeting."

"For us <u>all</u>? What do you mean?"

"Look. This traveler comes out of nowhere running so fast he hasn't thought about where he is. He's from the outside and probably dreads the idea of being here, let alone falling unprotected to sleep. He's probably just as unclear about all this as we are." Thodox was aggravated by Quei's need to examine everything. "I'll bet you that's exactly what we'll discover."

"We'll soon find out. All we have to do is go through there and over that ridge!"

Nothing more was said. They both took a look ahead and then at one another. They were almost at their destination. Each secretly hoped, as they set upon the last stretch, that what the Elders had privately said to each would not be needed. They also hoped that the Elders were correct in their selection of them to accomplish this task. Perhaps there were other better suited Dwellers for this venture!

Unknown to both Quei and Thodox, the Elders had not chosen them lightly. Even though the time had been short, a great amount of consideration and debate had led to the picking of their names before all finally agreed upon both. This had all been done before the convening, not to undermine the process, but rather to be ready if this was the consensus of the Dwellers. The Elders realized that together these two would have all the skills and talent needed to find and return safely with this traveler. Any unexpected danger could easily be handled by either of them. No other Dweller could be relied upon as confidently. Whether they knew it or not they were the best. All the same, the Chief Elder had spoken to each privately, providing some extra insurance if the worst was to ensue. Should the need arise, Quei and Thodox were well armed!

Chapter 4.

The land of Ice, or 'Ice Barrens' as it was known, lay to the distant north. It was both magnificent and cold. Lengths upon lengths of ice, covered its sub surface, which was at one time, warm, fertile and exposed. Now, and for as long as recent memory, its landscape was boundless in its icy blue glow. The distant foothills were the only markers of the beginning of the other worlds that lay beyond this solid flat tundra. It was a cruel place, tremendously harsh and unforgiving to the unprepared.

Few *lived* here; rather they existed and soon became hardened to their surroundings. After long enough exposure to these Barrens, the inhabitants: the Kith of the Ice, became addicted to the blueness of the atmosphere and found themselves unable to stay for extended periods in the more mellow outside worlds. Their eyes could not adjust to the differences in colors, and their bodies became progressively unable to readapt to outworld 'normal' time conceptualization.

The Kith were alien to all but themselves, in every way imaginable. All their traditions and practices, which were shaped by their icy environment, were unlike any outworlder's experience. They lived for the moment and were physical in their gratification. The inhabitants respected brutality as strength, seeing daily life as a series of challenges that you either won or lost. They held no middle ground in deed or argument. When they spoke it was brief and awkward. Their communication had fallen to basics, as it reflected a society which could not afford the luxury of ornamentation. They were forced to be utilitarian, and grew to like it. This combined with their 'addiction' to their harsh environment, made them permanent outcasts from the outworlds.

The Kith, though reveling in their isolation, disliked the way the outworlder imposed further alienation and increasingly, in an effort to rekindle self respect, began rejecting their rejecters. *Who were these outworlders to judge and dismiss?!* The transition to mercenary, in service to the outworlds, was noticeably short. The effect was one of continued isolation, to the point that the reasons that had created and developed this separation so long ago, were now themselves isolated and forgotten. All that remained was the sickening dislike for all the outworlds, except for the Gottlands. The Kith became what they disliked so much from the outworlds!

The Ice Barrens was the land of no night, just one incredible long twilight followed by new sunrises and twilight's and sunrises. The 'Riders', as they were seen to be and called in the outworlds, were really only from the part of the Kith making up the farthest northern inhabited section of the Ice Barrens. The outworlders didn't really know much and were not that well informed when it came to the subject of the North. The crazed behavior of the Kith or 'Riders', and their preference to the two tone darkness of evening when in the 'yellower' outworlds, was not understood. Unlike most of the Kith, these Riders tended to earn much of their fun and living from selling their services, and spent more time than any other of the Kith in the outworlds. The abundance and variety of color in the far South repulsed them just as much! As a result of their repulsion, they preferred, when not in the Ice Barrens, to deal with the drab ruggedness of the Gottlands, and the Gotts who lived in a similar way to that of the Riders. The Gotts were also not pursuers of the unnecessary 'things' that the southern worlds valued, and they did not, at least openly, display prejudices and disgust to the members of the Kith! It had been this way since the Old times.

It was to these Riders that Lord Merm turned again, after the conclusion of the southern invasion. This time not for their ability to find more slave labor, but to use their other skills! These Riders had proven most effective in the past. They would be able to track the thieves without drawing much attention, just as they had so efficiently found the female with her sword on the paths of the Forest. This renewed partnership with the Riders would be secretly negotiated. Even though it did not violate any terms of the newest peace with the South, Merm didn't want to cause alarm of any nature after the recent events.

Merm now needed to find Gorg. Gorg and his Six had returned home during the gaffufle between Troops and Jard Guard, in great disappointment. There wasn't any time to waste! Merm's lust for the power of the Magic was all consuming. While the South resumed its peaceful ways, Merm would re-focus his energies upon the Key. Once he could secure it, then he could re-think the process to the domination of the worlds. His immediate plan was to lull the South back into peace, while he surreptitiously pursued the magic! All he needed to know was which direction to follow and to where the thieves had escaped. He needed Gorg and his Six to help find the thieves, but first, he would have to find and make amends with Gorg!

During his disappearance after the cave-in at Norkleau, Merm's underlings had refused payment of the Riders reward. The Riders had been shunned, until finally they left disgusted for their home in the Ice Barrens. It would be difficult to entice them back into the service of the Lord, who had not paid. Merm would have to offer even more compensation to re-enlist their services. He felt lucky. He hoped his luck would last long enough to be able to have another chance at the Key!

But was it really luck? After the episode under the rubble of the Palace from which he had been pulled without serious injury, Merm was faintly aware of other 'supernatural' explanations to his drive, determination and rescue. He became trance-like while recalling the scene.

There had been a vision during the interval of his entrapment beneath the rocks. A strange glow of light and voice, a voice that was from both within and without. It was the same one as his dreams. It spoke with the reassurance of all knowing and calmed Merm's claustrophobic terror:

"You will not perish. We are with you and prevent harm. You must search for the thieves and reclaim the Key. It is the answer to all your questions and will make you invincible. Do not give up. All is *contained* and near to hand. Follow us and together we will achieve great magic!"

It was shortly after this voice that the digging of the Troopers revealed their Lord. Merm still was not clear if it was someone else's voice or just his own panicking thoughts during the emotional stress of the cave-in. There had been such a long silence and darkness. Not even the crying of the wounded or crushed was heard within his tight tomb. It was horrifying!

Merm had been trapped under a leaning part of the statue's GIANT leg. He was pinned against the wall, and the rest of the falling rubble had sealed him into that tiny air starved space. Before his total encasement, Merm thought he had seen the thieves crushed by the falling rock, but after his rescue, no trace was ever found of them or the prize! So much had passed so quickly. He had expected to perish!

Rmont was also alive, having been quick enough to make it to the passageway. His only injury: a broken arm. The two were together still. This heartened Merm, since he wasn't comfortable with the idea of continuing, after this calamity, solely on his own abilities. Yes, he had been lucky, but could he use this good fortune, and the Riders, to find the Key? Merm felt the skin around his neck where the instrument of magic had rested, as he contemplated his course of action for the time ahead. It all seemed to be a dream. He was in the castle room sitting at his large work table, and if it were not for the evidence of the broken wall as a verification that these events had ever happened, it would be too unreasonable to believe! This reminder of the theft enraged him. As he admonished himself for allowing the Key to be so easily taken, he grabbed its container, which had been left on the table. He considered the plainness of its design and marveled at the humbleness of such power. If it had been made for him, the container would have been much more richly adorned. Such a plainness could easily be thrown out as a piece of valueless junk! He played with the box as he brooded over the loss of its contents and in play opened its lid. He ran a large grimy finger over the inside surface, his mind still on the disappointment of the loss. Through his fingers he became aware of notches where smoothness was anticipated. His interest peeked. Bringing the box closer to view, he brushed lightly against the notched area with his dirty digit. As he brushed, more grime attached itself and began to disclose hieroglyphics. He rubbed more till all the symbols were clear. He began to read the message they gave. Sitting back in his chair the disappointment of moments before was replaced by great satisfaction. He knew most of the meaning of the symbols. He knew where to find the thieves!

- - - - - - - - - - - - - - - - - - -

Gorg and his Six had been infuriated when no reward was forthcoming after all their excursions and help to the Lord of the Gotts. They did not yet share Merm's satisfaction. In the chaos of the battle, the negotiations and the disappearance of the Lord Merm, no Gott considered payment necessary. As far as they were concerned, that was between the Riders and Lord Merm. It was not binding upon them. Instead of waiting to see where the dust would settle, Gorg left in disgust, feeling shunned by the Gotts. Next time it would be reward up front! There was nothing that could disturb a Rider more than to be cheated out of what was his due.

Another reason for their leaving was to try and distance themselves from any close connection with the Gotts, from the outworlder's point of view, especially since the 'invincible' Troops were beaten, and the long term outcome somewhat unclear. Gorg was taking no chances to be caught in the middle and risk some sort of punishment from the Jardian Guard! Even the Kith respected the reputation of the Guard. He did not want to give them any excuse for exacting compensation for their mercenary part against the South. By the time the ink was dry on the new treaty of peace, he and his Six were back secluded in the Ice Barrens. Unfortunately so was the Lord Merm, not in the Ice Barrens, but in Norkleau. Had the Riders waited, they would have been able to settle directly with Merm.

"Bad no reward paid. Do no more helpy Gotts!" Gorg was complaining to himself in his under surface ice den.

The Kith carved their homes out of the ice below the surface. Long, hand dug trenches led to squarely proportioned austere rooms. There was a fire in a corner and an ice chimney through which the blue smoke climbed its way to the tundra above. It was never very warm inside or out. There was little in terms of comfort, personal or stylistic. The beds, tables and chairs were carved out of a crystalline substance, and when they began to wear or crumble, were tossed out and new ones carved. In this 'home', Gorg continued his self reproachment. His mate, who dared not intrude in his upset, scurried around preparing the days end meal.

Merm was also having his meal prepared. He had asked that he and Rmont eat together in the castle room to discuss 'things'. Rmont could still be relied upon to be loyal after all the embarrassment with the loss in the South. He could barely wait to share his new discovery. A knocking came at the door and Rmont entered.

"My Lord, how pleased I am to find you!" This was the first time since the cave-in that Rmont had actually spoken with Merm. "I was so afraid that you...had...had... — been hurt," he didn't utter the word died.

"No, it will take more than a few stones! Come my old friend sit and let's talk." He indicated the table and the prepared food. This was another first for Rmont. Never had Merm treated him as an equal.

"Thank you my Lord." Rmont came down the stairs crossed to the table, and sat to the left of the head chair. Merm sat at the head. They started their meal, and Merm opened the conversation:

"We have been through much together and now it seems we are at an impasse. We came so close to obtaining what Lord Ho had once controlled. I am not speaking of the skirmish with the South, but the Key and the magic. I didn't tell you before, but this Key is spoken of in the Forbidden Books. With it, the possessor can procure great magic, a magic to compare to the Old times. I had hoped that we together could have surpassed Ho and rebuilt a strong Empire." His tone was very cordial, causing Rmont to question what was coming next.

"Yes Lord. It is sad that we have been stopped so soon. If only we could do more!" Rmont realized as he spoke why the Lord Merm and he were together. Merm had a plan. This was not the stopping point.

"There is something *we* can do. *We* must travel to the North and get the help of the Riders to track and capture the thieves. The problem is, I must remain here in Norkleau until the eyes of the South are turned away from the Gottlands. I need a reliable Gott to go to the Ice Barrens and secure the help of the Riders."

"But Lord. Their reward was not given. They will not welcome any Gott in their land."

"An oversight, you could go to deliver the reward and offer a bonus if they will continue to serve. Tell Gorg that they should have waited, that the reward was waiting and...well you are better at diplomacy than I. You have saved us before. I need you to go. You are the only one I can trust. We must not give up on this second chance. We must find the Key!"

"But what if they are not willing?"

"Here look at this." Merm put his hand in his pocket and pulled out the box that had held the Key.

"What is it?" Rmont took the small container and shrugged.

"It is the box that we together removed from the hiding place. Look inside."

Rmont lifted the lid and examined the box.

"I don't understand?"

"Look closely! Do you see?!" Merm was excited and agitated at the length of time it was taking Rmont to discover what even he had originally overlooked. "Do you see?"

Rmont strained his eyes. What was it? What could he not see that Merm had?

"On the bottom, under there." Merm pointed and directed Rmont's visual search. "See?"

Suddenly it was revealed! It was so incredibly simple!

"But Lord! How could we have missed such an obvious thing! When the Riders see this they will..." Merm cut in:

"Exactly! Go to the Riders, and tell them. This is providence. We are not far off! We need their help one last time, and with this box we are assured success. How foolish of the thieves to leave such a thing behind. We will be a step ahead of them now!"

Both broke into a joyous laughter as this new ray of

hope was now laid open. The animosity and distrust that each held for the other was temporarily put aside. If only they had noticed before! They would finish their meal and then Rmont would take a lone horse and hurry to the Riders; a new energy and faith burning brightly in his greedy soul.

With the discovery of the secret in the box, the Magic was as close as the time it would take Merm, Rmont and the Riders to join together and pursue the thieves. Merm would join them as soon as he could slip away unnoticed. The answer had been on their doorstep all along. It had been waiting to be claimed by the first passer by. Merm intended to be the first, but he still required the aid of the Riders of the Kith.

- - - - - - - - - - - - - - - - - -

Gorg was still angry and non-communicative. It was the time for food. He kept complaining about the loss of reward. His mate knew better than to interfere in this and merely carried on.

"Eat now. Late it is." She pushed a round object at him. It was a bread hollowed out to form a type of multipurpose plate and bowl. She ladled in a stew and Gorg slurped down the food. After the stew was eaten he ripped at the bread till there was no plate either.

"Food good." He belched so loud the place almost shuddered. This was considered well mannered!

"More want?"

"Naw." He grunted, and a smile came over his face. He gazed 'that look' into his mate's eyes. She knew what it meant. He got up and grabbed hold of her while she feigned a protest. He pulled her to their bed area. They fell to the bedding upon the cold floor and like an animal he began to take her. She responded, knowing that by giving into this brutality she would be helping him to forget a far greater atrocity: the disappointment and disgrace of returning to the Kith without payment by the Gotts of the promised reward. She hoped that her 'giving' to Gorg would in his mind begin to rekindle his confidence as the leader of his Six. Whatever was wrong she would help to make him feel better. It was her duty. They fell asleep wrapped amongst the bundle of their clothing and fur skinned bedding.

- - - - - - - - - - - - - - - - - - - -

Rmont had ridden through the darkness of the Gottlands to the blue twilight of the Ice Barrens. He carried the reward and a tracing of the hieroglyphics from the box on a piece of paper. The ancient writing would help convince the Riders of the truth should they doubt his words. It was a depressing half light. His eyes were already aching from the color depravation. The sooner he could be out of this place the better!

He had gone north west from Norkleau to a district east of the uppermost corner of the Burning Forest. It had no particular name, but was the residence for the Kith at this time of season. He would seek the rising smoke that came from the dens under the ice. There he would find the Riders and Gorg.

It was at the cross point between twilight and sunrise when Rmont finally came upon the correct locale. There were several stacks of smoke rising up then flowing horizontally to the ice. Rmont's breath obscured his vision. He quickly understood to blow it in the opposite direction of his view. Stopping his ride, he considered which den to disturb. He didn't appreciate that his choices had already been made.

"Move not. Careful or dead be!" It was Tan, and Tan knew that this was not just a Gott, but the Gott who advised the Lord Merm. He could tell by the special insignia placed on Rmont's uniform. He also had a strong memory for faces and remembered this one as the one that had caused him embarrassment over the loss of the female. This, coupled with the lack of reward, put Rmont in a tenuous position.

"I come to see Gorg. The Lord Merm sends greeting." Rmont used his experience to bluff his way past this dirty inferior. "Take me to Gorg!" It was not a question.

"Merm dead is. Under rock lie. No reward give!" Tan was not pleasant. He would not harm the Gott since the standing order was to present all to the Head Rider of the Six. He could play, however, with this Gott a little before he took him to Gorg.

"The Lord is sad Gorg left without his reward. I am here to offer it with a bonus." He indicated the heavy looking bag to his left side. This opportunity to please his Head Rider changed the way Tan was thinking.

"Reward here? Gorg pleased be. I take. Down get." Though the hour was early he would disturb Gorg. Tan realized how this good news would return all to a better mood.

Rmont got slowly to ground level and undid the bag. Tan attempted to take hold of it.

"This is to be given by my hands to Gorg. Lord Merm has commanded me." Rmont challenged the Rider. There was a tense moment after which Tan grunted and led him off to the den of Gorg.

As they walked, the sound of boots squeaking on ice was the only sound to be heard. There were no other sentries. In fact, Tan just happened to be up relieving himself when he had heard the sound of the approaching outworlder upon the ice tundra. He had carefully climbed out of his den and up the several lengths to the surface. After scanning the area, he identified the lone Gott. They were unmistakable in size and lack of stealth when traversing the worlds. How simple it had been to surprise him.

They both walked to the fourth column of smoke and Tan beckoned Rmont to follow him down the long carved-out grade to the den below.

"Gorg here is." Tan re-assessed Rmont, "Sleep

does. Better true be!" Before he continued he was checking to make certain this was not a trick. Rmont stared him straight in the eyes.

"I am not here to waste anyone's time! Get on with it!" Rmont was tiring of this oaf's questioning and idle threats.

With that, Tan brusquely knocked his shoulder into Rmont as he proceeded down the grade. Rmont followed, both of their exhaling breaths rising out like steam and partially obscuring them as the sight of their backs dipped below the icy surface.

Gorg was awake, relaxed and still aggravated about the reward. His mate curled up beside him in a half sleep. The den was cool with little warmth coming from the tiny embers of the remaining fire. He contemplated the emptiness.

Tan and Rmont had gone down the grade and were now under the ice in a carved tunnel. It was cramped for a Gott; being about three lengths in height and two lengths in width, but it allowed the Rider to pass without discomfort. There was no light but that which reflected through the opening of the tunnel and the translucency of the ice. The tunnel was cut straight and other than the smooth four surfaces nothing came to notice. Tan stopped in front of what was to Rmont, just a wall. This was the entrance to Gorg's den. Upon closer scrutiny Rmont realized that it was a doorway. There were straight cut marks, which were almost invisible as they blended in with the dim glow and the rest of the ice, this was the area of the entrance.

Tan, after giving Rmont one last glare, announced loudly:

"Gorg! Tan wait. Outworlder Gott come!" There was no knocking, only the sound of the words. "Gorg! Open ."

Rmont was struck by the abruptness and lack of deference to a superior. Tan waited for some sort of response. If this was done to Merm, especially when interrupted from private quarters and rest—it was inconceivable!

Gorg heard the announcement. He rose from his bed pushing his mate aside without care.

"What want? Why me bother!" He picked up a weapon as assurance, before pulling on his crumpled clothing.

"Tan wait! Gott from Merm come. Bring reward!"

With the mention of reward and the Lord Merm, Gorg's suspiciousness lessened and he more rapidly prepared.

"Merm? Reward? Wait. Me come." He buttoned up his outer jacket, then opened the door by pulling the leather strap on the right side. Without a noise the doorway opened. Gorg was menacingly ready. There before him stood Tan and an ugly Gott. The ugly Gott was the advisor of Merm. The one who had been present at his meeting in Norkleau with the Gotts' Lord. It was this one who had suggested to Merm what course to take after the loss of the female, causing extra effort and increased risk. Gorg disliked and did not trust him. He remembered him well.

Rmont also remembered and felt uncomfortable. The tables had changed and now he was in the inferior position, having to be careful lest the anger of Gorg be released upon him. He was outnumbered and at the mercy of this Rider. It was not a position Rmont wanted to become used to, but he would not display these insecurities. He had a duty to perform. An unnoticed touch of the bag of reward rekindled his nerve.

The moment Gorg saw the Gott, but not the bag, his frustration let go and he pounced upon the larger Rmont backing him out against the tunnel's ice wall.

"Where reward is?! Merm word bad!" He had a grip on Rmont. "You give or no go back!" Rmont was ruffled.

"Hold on! The reward is here!" he indicated the bag and threw in, "Even with a bonus as a sign of our valuation of our brothers of the Kith." He used the familiar correct calling. "This last while has been confusing, but not in our faith and respect for the Kith! Accept this reward with our gratitude."

Rmont's strength of speech had calmed the Rider. He handed the bag to Gorg. Gorg backed away with the bag. Tan followed after him, huddling close and peering over Gorg's shoulder. After opening it Gorg was pleased. His mood now swung to content. He pushed the eager Tan to one side, away from reach of the bag of reward. As he did he admonished Tan. This was more for the benefit of the Gott than a chastising of the rider.

"See, tell you did reward come. That Gott good!" Gorg was putting on his best show for Rmont as he spoke out to Tan. "Get rest. We guest have of Merm." Tan was dismissed to gather the rest of the community for a celebration of the reward and entertainment of this official visitor. He bowed as he left Rmont. This was a ceremonious gesture of respect. They were *friends* again!

"Welcome to Kith. Me Gorg. You at castle. We celebrate now." Gorg was informing Rmont, who he did not know by name, in the formal ways of the Kith in accepting a reward. This outward display was one of the rare times of ceremony.

"I am Rmont, advisor to Lord Merm." He bowed in the required formality, "Before everybody is here, could we talk in more," he hesitated and by motion implied, "*private a* place? It is a little difficult to talk here in the cold and I have something else to ask of the Kith."

Gorg squinted his eyes and gave more serious attention.

"What more have?"

"Not here. There is something else," Rmont paused, "of great value!"

Gorg considered briefly then in an acknowledging way directed:

"We go. Come. More silent be." He started to walk further into the tunnel, Rmont in tow.

It all looked the same to Rmont: four icy smooth surfaces, no doors or lights, other than the blue glow within the ice. There must have been some sort of light source hidden within the ice somewhere, but it was not obviously placed. Rmont's eyes ached, he rubbed one then the other. Gorg commented: "Eyes change, take time. We give drink to helpy." With that Gorg pushed against a portion of the ice and it opened into a large room. It was clearly a meeting place for the Kith. No-one was present. Only rows of translucent benches and the odd table. At the front was a larger table and a larger bench. Everything was placed to resemble a semi-circular conference center. Gorg walked in and sat on the large bench; Rmont beside him.

"Here safe is. Talk private can." Gorg was awaiting the conversation, he was intrigued and reasoned to himself that there might be great personal reward. There was no need to let all the Riders know *all* the details! Rmont put his hand into his pocket carefully, so as not to alarm Gorg. Gorg watched and was clearly mesmerized. Rmont removed his hand and placed the tiny piece of paper up on the table between them.

"The answer to our mutual desires lies here!" Rmont smiled and leaned back leaving the paper on the table. Gorg wasn't sure if he should laugh or again become infuriated.

"What this be! Child game! How can helpy?"

"Pick it up and have a look." Rmont was under orders from Merm not to educate the Riders in the magic. He was to interest the greedy Riders by reward. He knew Gorg and his Six were motivated by profit. He was to tell Gorg of the female and the stealing of a thing of great value from the Lord of the Gotts. Merm wanted it back, it was his. The Lord would reward as never before, upon its return.

"Just paper is. What you do? Make silly of Gorg?!" Gorg had little humor nor understanding of jokes and did not like the direction that this was following. Rmont, understanding Gorg's asperity, continued:

"Look closer! See the tracings?", Gorg saw the traced symbols, but didn't see the point, "Take a look and tell me what you see." Rmont was developing the mystery as if speaking with a child. Gorg saw the symbols.

"What mean signs?"

"These tell of the *valuable* stolen from Lord Merm. These tell of the place where the thieves will go." Rmont's excitement infected Gorg, "It is not too late to recover the *valuable*; the *valuable* your labor helped to uncover. The Lord Merm will be very thankful to any who would now help. He is not able to leave at this time to do it himself. The South watches his every step. They dislike and wish to destroy the ones in the North!" Rmont exaggerated, playing on the animosity between the Kith and the rest of the worlds, "They are behind the stealing and hope to keep the reward to themselves. It will give them power. Power to control..." He trailed off and checked to see if his tale had hooked the Rider.

"What power it be?" Gorg was concerned. The mention of the South had convinced him of the importance of helping the Gotts.

"The power to conquer the North. To make all live like the South. They must be stopped! We must not let them reach Tika and the hiding place of the Key, before us! Their abilities already threaten the North. We have just seen the beginning of their power by their attack of the Gottlands! The Kith will be next!"

"Why they attack?"

"They wanted to distract us so that they could steal from Lord Merm a Key to unlock the reward. We are lucky to have found the symbols and their secret. Now together, we will be able to arrive first and stop the thieves of the South from obtaining the power of the reward. The Gotts and the Kith are in great peril. We need to help one another before it is too late. The South is already ahead." Rmont was pleased with the manipulation of Gorg, "What will the brave Riders of the Kith do?"

There was a stillness. Gorg studied the paper once more. The symbols were of a language unknown to him. Their presence was an uneasiness to him. He had wondered why the Gottlands and outworlders had fought. This information of Rmont's was possible, almost to be expected. He must join with the Lord Merm and prevent the outworlders from threatening the North and the Kith. He also realized there would be great profit for all!

"Put to the Six. The Six decide." Gorg, in the way of the Kith, would put the offer before the Riders. It was their way. Once the Head Rider was convinced to put an offer forward, it almost guaranteed the agreement of the remaining Riders. It was another formality amongst them, seldom refused but required in terms of traditions. Although the Riders were an unkempt unruly sect, in truth, they were organized and acted in many ways like any other society.

Gorg's mate, without prompting, arrived with a tray and primitive cups. A steaming kettle containing some sort of hot liquid was placed in the middle. She entered and then left, after putting the beverage upon the table in front of the two. Gorg was silent. Riders never spoke of business in front of their mates. When she had gone, he offered:

This helpy eye." He used a finger to point to Rmont's eyes, "Drink now. Soon together we go." This was Gorg's way of letting Rmont know that this was just a ceremony that needed to be observed.

"Thank you." Rmont lifted the mug to his lips and sniffed, then drank the steaming fluid, "I drink to our joining."

The drink was sweet, with the hint of something bitter. It went down and warmed his cold body. Gorg seemed pleased that the Gott was enjoying this mug. Not long after, Rmont thought the aching was diminishing, or was it just that he was getting used to it. In any event he felt better and drank more.

The voice of Tan came to the entrance of the meeting room. He had informed and returned with all the Riders and they were assembled in the tunnel. They would enter only after the proper announcement had been made.

"Six, that one make, wait. Enter now and question bring. All will be speak. All will decide."

With that said they all filed in and took places on the semi-circle ice benches. The entrance was closed. Gorg stood up.

"Rmont of Gottland bring reward has. Travel of Lord Merm does. We thank." There was a general agreeing moan, "Ask more does. Much profit. Outworlders cause harm. Want Six helpy. What say?" It was open to the Riders and each in his turn by custom must speak to the question. Tan being the second commenced.

"Why helpy? What need Kith now Gotts? Then the next:

"When reward given?" And...

"Why Gotts need Kith?

They discussed and finally it was time for Rmont to appeal to them, as was the convention.

"Lord Merm sends me to ask for the help of the Kith. You are North ones with us. We need to join together to stop the South from profiting from our disunion. Together we are stronger. The Gottland is weakened," he did not go into all the details as he had with Gorg, "There is nowhere to turn except to our brothers here. True, we have had our arguments, but they only make us stronger. Help again; now to stop the South!" All this was formality, since at the end Gorg would stand and accept for the Kith. Rmont sat down. Tan rose again, this time out of turn.

"What female with sword is?"

Rmont was caught off guard. What did this Rider mean? Did he know of the magic? Looking over at Gorg he noticed a new suspicion lingering in the air.

"Why do you ask?"

"Want know!"

Rmont wanted to avoid trouble without giving anything away. "The female was a thief from the South. She," he paused then realized a way out that would convince the Riders to join, "she has stolen the sword of the Lord. It is ancient and is a symbol of the Gotts. The South is trying to fragment us. By taking the sword they will hold the legal right to rule the Gottlands. They will give the sword to enemies who dwell in the Forest. They claim right of rule. With the sword, it will be hard to stop their claim. We must get the *valuable* back!"

The Riders gave out hoots and boos. They did not like those that dwelled in the Forest, and believed what Rmont said as plausible. They would have to join with the Lord Merm to stop the outworlders!

Gorg said nothing about this new story from Rmont. He didn't care if the Six knew the *real* reason or not, he would rather save the reward that this Key would unlock for himself, letting the Six recover only the sword if one existed. Everyone would be happy. He would keep the extra profit, or as he was beginning to think, split it with Rmont. There was something funny about this Gott that did not ring entirely true. Gorg felt it was probably the fact that Rmont was being underhanded, but he could respect that since there was nothing wrong with an underling attempting to rise up. If the leader was fool enough to allow this to happen, then obviously it was a sign of the weakness of the one in charge. It was only natural for this to be discovered and corrected by placing another more capable and more shrewd in charge! He rose up again and all in the room became still.

"We hear much. Time now we join Lord Merm. Must save North." This signaled the Riders to shout and begin the celebrations of reward and new venture. In the noise Gorg leaned over to Rmont and with a boyish grin said:

"Six get sword. Two get Key to reward!"

Rmont wondered if Gorg realized what it all meant. He grinned back. His mission was accomplished!

Chapter 5.

Under the great Moonfruit they stood resting; the journey was through. It had been a long night, and with the approach of the early dew, Quei and Thodox took a moment to admire the still beauty. Quei leaned forward placing his hand upon the bark of Fon and looked up into the higher branches. There, still under the sleep induced by both the Moonfruit and fatigue, was the traveler. Thodox had also spotted him.

"Old friend," Quei directed his words quietly to Fon. "It is good to be here with you again. We have come for this one. It is time to release him from your hold." Quei waited to 'sense' the response. It was long in coming. There was an empathy to be felt and Quei was a little out of practice when communing with the Moonfruit. Gradually the message was put together by Fon.

"How good to once again feel your presence. We are full of blossom in your greeting." This was the way in which Fon communed. As there was no gender for the Moonfruit it spoke in it's language through the 'sense' and the touch of it's bark. The vibrations were transferred to the one who touched. This was easier for Quei who was unpracticed in the skill of pure sensing. There were those amongst the Dwellers who could interpret the pure communing of the Pine, but they were specialized in their abilities by many years of experience. Quei and Thodox, being mere beginners, relied on the physical contact to communicate. "Up in the arms of us lies the traveler. It is most different, and reminds the Pine of one before!"

"One before?" Quei was intrigued. "What do you mean?"

"Long ago, one such as this passed our wood. It was of great power and we had little effect upon. It was of great age. It traveled to the home of the Ones from before. We gave passage without harm, and none befell us. This traveler is of the same origin." Fon was slow in communing to Quei. Old Moonfruit never were in a hurry. They thought and spoke as they existed, in a very considered and gradual way. "It is in danger and in flight. It only entered our wood after great fear. It is being sought by something of which it is uncertain. This could be 'sensed' by us in our probing, but we were unable to penetrate far. There is a power of the Old Ones within it. We also begin to fear the reason for its entry. We see danger following swiftly! There is not much time before it is upon us and we are again threatened from the worlds not of the Pine." Fon stopped and awaited Quei's response.

Quei took a moment and retold what he had learned from Fon to Thodox. Thodox commented:

"This is reminiscent of the stories of the early times, when the Old Ones of the Palace beneath the Stars helped the Dwellers and all those of the Forest from the *Evil* and greed of the other places. It seems that this traveler is in need of something. We had better wake him and find out what is going on out there. Maybe he can explain the recent darkness in the skies above." Thodox suddenly considered that the recent overcast heavens could have been more than just unusual stormy weather. Dwellers only concerned themselves with those activities of the non Forest world that directly could have some immediate impact upon them. As a result they were not aware of the recent attack of the Gotts upon the South, only the darkness above!

Quei after a moment of reflection, continued his communing with Fon: "This is useful knowledge for us. We thank the Pine. Now, you must release the traveler."

"But we do not control it. That is what worries us. The traveler was only under our influence at the beginning. As it slept and regained strength we lost our dominance. It is of great power and is protected by other sources! It will awaken when it decides to awaken."

"Well, we will speed up the process," Quei pulled back from the bark and motioned to Thodox. "Thod," as he called him for short, "Climb up and give our traveler a cheery good sunrise."

Thodox smiled while he removed his waist belt and placed his long walking stick against the trunk of Fon. He looked upward while rubbing his hands together: "This shouldn't take long. Maybe I should also bring some root tea with biscuits!" He joked and then stretched one arm up to the first branch as it was lowered by Fon. Quci watched both Thodox climb and the traveler sleep.

During the conversation between Fon and the Dwellers on the forest floor, Julian had been rapidly awakening from his deep rest. The voice of his father was shaking him: *"Waken, my son, friends arrive. You must greet them as a Stoneman. Tell them you are a Keeper. That you run from the Palace of the Old Ones. Ask for their help and they will take you to Buold the head elder of the Dwellers. He knows of your coming, as it has been revealed through the ritual of the Dwellers dream this night. You will know by talking to him, where to hide the Key and the Passwords. You will not tell him of these or your purpose, but he will realize the meaning of your speech. It was placed in his mind long ago and passed on from generation to generation. It is the promise of the Dwellers to the Old Ones. He will speak of where you need to go. You will understand at the moment of telling."*

Thodox was almost upon Julian, when at that instant

the traveler awakened. Julian's sudden movement as he opened his eyes and stretched, startled Thodox to the point that he lost his balance and fell the short distance to the ground. With a soft thud he landed upon the loam, unharmed. Quei broke out in laughter. The obvious innocence on the part of the traveler simply awakening, and the extreme caution of Thodox not knowing what to expect was humorous. There was no danger. Just two startled looks.

"Wooooo! What the!" Was all that was heard as Thodox fell.

Julian also yelled out in response to the sudden sight of Thodox looming over top of him in the tree and about to touch him to wake him up: "Hey! Wha…at the!"

In the end Thodox was grumbling on the ground; the traveler was peering down, and Quei was bent over in gut ripping laughter! This displeased Thodox more as he rose from the dirt and brushed himself off.

"What's so funny! Didn't you ever see anyone fall before?" Thodox frowned, not liking a joke at his expense!

In between contortions caused by the laughter Quei blurted: "You…looked…so…start…led! That…way you jumped…it was…so…so," he couldn't control the laugh as he recalled the image, "…so…" The words were lost in the chuckle.

"Oh shut up! It could happen to anyone. How did I know he would jump at me like that!"

Julian peered down and saw the two characters. He said nothing. Soon, as if the dumbness had power, both Quei and Thodox also fell silent and met the gaze of Julian.

"Hello. I am Quei and this is Thodox. We are of the Forest Dwellers. We have been sent to greet you and invite you to our home. Will you join us?"

"I am a Keeper, a Stoneman. There is a great *Evil* that follows after me. Any who are near me may also convoke its anger. It is fair that you know of these things." Julian's tone was stern. Even as he spoke, he noticed his compelling seriousness.

"We thank you, but we still invite you to follow us and rest in the safety of our home." Quei motioned with his right arm the Forest around them, "Even these great Pines are more than they appear. There are many eyes and ears here. It will be difficult to bring harm to any friend of the Forest."

"Yes, we are here because we were informed by the eyes and ears of the Forest of your entry. You have been under close scrutiny since last sun setting." Thodox was trying to corroborate what Quei had said.

"Will you take me to *Buold* ?"

Both of the Dwellers were astounded by this apparent knowledge of the traveler about their oldest and wisest Elder. They stood and began to question the traveler's knowledge. Julian did not hear a word that they said. He was distracted by an inner voice:

"Are you of the other who once passed this way?" Fon who hadn't wanted to reveal the abilities of the Pine spoke through sense to Julian, catching him off guard.

"Who's that?!" Julian wasn't aware of the Moonfruit as he thought the response.

"Are you of the other?" repeated Fon.

"Who is speaking?!" Julian panicked and spoke out loud, thinking it might be the *Evil*.

Below, Quei and Thodox realizing that the traveler had not been listening to them, but to something else, understood the source of the communication. They were astounded that this traveler was able to 'sense' the Moonfruit. Gradually they got Julian's attention and answered his '*who is speaking*' question. They took turns finishing each other's phrases: "It is Fon. The Moonfruit you are in. It speaks through 'sense' and the touching of its bark, to whomever it chooses. It is one of the eyes and ears we spoke of before."

Julian concentrated, then in his mind connected with

the Moonfruit without allowing the Dwellers to hear: "I am a Keeper, the Stoneman's Son. Who asks?"

"I am called Fon. I remember the other. It was a long time in the past. Do not concern yourself with us. We owe much to the Old Ones of whom you are a part. We will help."

"How are you aware of all this?" continued Julian as Quei and Thodox watched the scene of the concentrating but not speaking Keeper.

"We have come close to you and spoken with the other. We will not harm, but honor. Go with these two. They will help you find what you need to know."

Without understanding why, Julian broke out of his concentration and stopped the communication. Fon's last 'sensing' to Julian was quickly transferred and clearly let him know that they would be meeting again before all this had concluded. Julian picked up where he had left off with the Dwellers, "I will come, but you must help me down! It was easier getting up!"

"Careful," Thodox cautioned. What had happened to him might also happen to the Stoneman, "one falling is enough for this sun rising!"

The mood of the three had changed from apprehensive to friendly. Thodox re-climbed the great Moonfruit to assist Julian. Quei remained below. Soon they were all standing next to Fon's trunk shaking hands and re-introducing themselves.

"How do you know the name *Buold* ?" Quei questioned, "Have you been here before?"

"Yes, how do you know?" Thod was interested.

"I cannot tell you, but it is necessary that I am taken swiftly to him. It is important for *all* of our futures. He expects my coming and can explain further. We should go soon. My pursuers are close behind."

"Fine," Quei pensively changed the topic. "We can leave now and be back in the Dwelling by highest sun. Are you up for the trip?"

"Oh yes, my purpose will carry me on. Let's go!"

As they started the return, Julian gave one searching

scan of the route behind. He wondered when the *Evil* of Merm would catch up with him. He felt it near. Its chilliness approached. Would he be able to hide the Key and protect the *Passwords* from their grasp? He found and gripped the two red books tighter, in an attempt to reassure himself that all was secure. They must hurry!

- - - - - - - - - - - - - - - - - - -

The *Evil* was not far behind, but it wasn't Merm. It was Dorluc! Julian was not yet aware of this power behind Merm and he was not cognizant of the scope of the threat that pursued. Only Darla and the nephews knew, and unlike Julian, were now being more circumspect so as not to alert the *Evil* to their location or plans. Julian was still growing in his use of the Magic and without realization, by its use, was targeting himself more rapidly.

Dorluc had kept scanning the worlds after the confrontation with the three in Jard. Now that he was revealed to them, they would shield their activities and guard their use of the Magic. The Key was not on them, but it wasn't yet hidden. He could tell by the fluctuation within the Magic; a fluctuation beyond the capabilities of these novice intruders to his plan. He turned to the view screen to hopefully capture another glimpse and gain information as to the place where the Key was currently being concealed. In doing so he noticed that the view screen was hovering around the Burning Forest. In and out of focus it went till eventually it stopped on an old large Pine. There it remained for the longest time. All that could be seen was the large Pine surrounded by smaller ones, nothing else. Dorluc sat mystified! Why had the view screen identified this as a source of drain? He was not as quick to discard the presentation, now that it was clear that the screen was working. He sat, and as it was dark, decided to wait till more light illuminated the picture and perhaps the reason for it to display an otherwise meaningless sight.

After waiting what seemed an eternity on the same scene, Dorluc witnessed the arrival of Quei and Thodox. The view screen was transfixed to this setting, and still Dorluc couldn't comprehend the reason. It was only when the sun had risen and the traveler was revealed in the branches, that he realized what was happening.

"There look! It is the same Jardian that we saw before. Why would he be in the Forest with the Dwellers?" These thoughts were spoken out loud though no-one else was in the room with him. He studied the scene and then noticed that attached to the Jardian was one of the red books. It was a book of the *Passwords*! At last it was within his reach! His *Evil* master would be impressed with the speed of the locating of the magic words. Dorluc would now muster up all the help he could, including that of the Lord Merm. It was clear that he must hurry to the Burning Forest and apprehend this Jardian, before the Dwellers could hide him away. He decided to influence Merm once again and direct him to the Books, and the Key that must also be concealed on the Jardian! Before that though, he would inform his master of the discovery; perhaps he could also be of assistance.

Turning his eyes from the scene under the old Pine, he called out: "Wakan, Wakan, my master I have news of the *Passwords*." Within an instant a blue white opaque cloud formed, and through it a face became half clear.

"The *Passwords*? Explain." Wakan paused, the sound of his deep raspy voice lingering.

"I have found the location of the thief with the magic. He is with the Dwellers. The others are still in Jard, but they do not possess the Key or the Books. It will be easy for us to stop this lone South Worlder and then use the power.

"Uhmm...This is more like you. Now hurry and

don't miss this opportunity. We must have the Magic in our grasp soon. There is an awakening started. Others will soon interfere."

"Thank you...I will not waste any time on this attempt. They will be ours!"

"Good. I am pleased, but don't disappoint me, or..." Wakan did not have to finish. Dorluc knew that failing this time would be hazardous to the chances of attaining escape from his imprisonment. Wakan had great power and could silence him forever.

Just as quickly as Wakan had appeared, he disappeared. Dorluc called out for his compatriots. One by one they entered the room.

"I have located the thief with the stolen items. It is to the home of the Dwellers that we must direct our allies. It must be done right away. Prepare yourselves, for we together will move Merm to complete our task." There was a general acknowledgment by those present. All were pleased with this turn of events. It would not be long till the Magic could be used to release them all from this land of no form!

- - - - - - - - - - - - - - - - - -

"Why is it that the return trip always seems faster?" Thodox was thinking out loud and did not want a response.

Both he and Quei were impressed with the agility of this traveler, no matter how peculiar he seemed. They had not stopped to rest, but made straight for their home deep within the western Forest. This traveler, who had not yet offered any name, was driven by something very frightening, or had power that wasn't obvious when seeing his outward appearance! He had not uttered a word all the way. He just kept looking over his shoulder every now and again, as if he was expecting something close behind which was following, but this was not of their concern. Their task was to retrieve and bring safely this traveler from the lower

Forest to the Elders. He was not even required to be blindfolded! This was unheard of. Only the Chosen of the ancient lore had been exempted. Never had a 'South Worlder' been allowed to see the paths to the Dwellers'! Quei and Thodox though confused and concerned knew better than to question the wisdom of the Elders. There must be a reason why the Elders hadn't insisted on the blindfolding. All three continued the trip. They were almost home.

- - - - - - - - - - - - - - - - - -

Dorluc had watched part of the female and two young ones' return journey from the safety of the view screen and his formless realm. How he longed to have physical form once again. Soon, he felt, his spiritual existence would change. He needed to find the *Passwords* to accomplish this end. He had decided to follow these three Jardians as far as he spiritually could, then influence Merm to send a party after them. He felt smug in his ability to track using the screen, without the awareness of the prey!

- - - - - - - - - - - - - - - - - -

Suddenly and without warning Julian stopped dead in mid step. Quei and Thodox were several lengths ahead before noticing.

"What's wrong?" Quei asked.

Julian stood still and shushed them both to be silent. "We are being watched!"

"Watched? By whom, where?" Thodox was tired of this game.

"We are being watched and followed. It must not find your home." Julian turned about and spoke in a strange language, to the openness. The two Dwellers, seeing and hearing no threat, became worried, and signaling each other, questioned the sanity of this Stoneman.

As Julian spoke his words, he began to circle and circle around upon the same spot, it made the onlookers dizzy. His speed increased and then, poof—he was gone!

- - - - - - - - - - - - - - - - - - -

Dorluc was as alarmed as were the two Dwellers. What had happened? He cursed as the picture faded. The view screen had been adjusted by Dorluc to seek and only track forces that could cause a drain on the Magic. Now that the drain, Julian, was gone, it did not remain on a scene that it believed contained none of this criteria The view screen changed to another visual of somewhere else. "No. Wait!" But the view screen continued its search.

- - - - - - - - - - - - - - - - - - -

Thodox was first to speak. "Where'd he go? What will we do now? Strange little guy wasn't he?"

"Uh uh." Was all that came from Quei's stunned being.

"Should we wait or go back or..." Thodox moved to Quei hoping for direction.

"I suggest that we continue on." Came a voice from nowhere. Julian's voice was clearly recognizable, but he was not!

"What manner of trickery is this," Quei was not pleased, "Who are you? Where are you?"

"Just what is going on?!" Thod was bewildered.

"I am here," Julian was still invisible to sight, "we were being watched by that which follows after me. He is able to locate me, but only when I am visible." Julian was not certain how he knew this, but in the panic he did. He wasn't even sure who the someone was, but deep within him he had an inexplicable intuition about something and he realized the dangers, "He does not know that this illusion will prevent him, for a

time, from being able to track me. I am only strong
enough to withstand a short period before I must re-
materialize. He will again find us. We must continue
quickly and prepare for what will soon come. How far
is there to go?"

"Not far," Quei heard his words answer though his
body remained dazed from these events, "We can be
there by the highest Sun. What is going on?" he again
asked, "Who are you and what is this *Evil* that pursues
you?"

"That is only for the ears of Buold. Please, good
Dwellers of the Forest, let us waste no more time. The
hope of each of our worlds depends upon my speedy
meeting with Buold." Julian was trying to secure their
confidence. He decided to be more personal, "My
name is Julian. I am of Jard. I am a Stoneman. All of
this is known by Buold. Please deliver me to him, before it is too late for all of us."

"If it was not for our orders to return with you, we
would leave you now," Quei saw Thod nod in agreement, "Before we go on I ask you for more proof of
what you say. How are we to believe your claims? It
might be a trick. Maybe you are the only threat! We
have not yet witnessed any of this *Evil* from which
you run. The only unusualness about is you! How
can you expect us to continue to believe you? We are
not used to meeting Southworlders, especially ones we
cannot see. What manner of creature are you? It was
conveyed to us through our Elders and legends that
one day one such as you may come through the Forest
and ask for our help. This was all agreed long ago. It
is also said that the 'ones' who travel, will not be
alone. He would carry great mysteries and know
words of promise, *Passwords* if you will, that would
establish and bind the assistance, as agreed by the
Dwellers in the Forest long ago. I am confused. If
you are what you say and have come this way in need
of that help, you will understand of what I am speaking. I am entitled to ask. Do you have any words that

will act as a sign of verification?" Quei waited. Both he and Thod were told to question for this special sign only if the situation demanded. There was no need to inquire unless obvious suspicion of the traveler existed in their minds.

According to the Elders, if this traveler was truly what he said he was, then by the oldest legends he would willingly comply. This would be the sign of a true Keeper of the Balance. Quei and Thod had been told to check if the need arose, and if the answer was not correct, to protect the Dwellers' secret home in the Forest, by dispatching the traveler. Otherwise Quei and Thodox were to return with this traveler without question, unless the situation became unusual, though unusual was not defined to them by the Elder who had spoken to each before they left to find this traveler.

The Elder had been Buold. In the event of unusual circumstances they were to ascertain the true intent of the visit of the traveler. If he was connected to the ones of the Palace, as might be the case as indicated by Fon, then they must quickly and safely return home, all three of them! Both Quei and Thodox glared in the direction of Julian's voice as they pondered their next move. It would be impossible to slay an enemy you couldn't see!

Long ago, when the Old Ones had protected the Dwellers and elicited their promise to aid any who carried the proper sign and could offer verification, it had been decided that any who were truly in the service of the people of the Palace, would be associated with, and know, as a password, the number three. If the traveler was alone, once the answer to a particular question was given as three, passage and protection would be granted. What this number meant or why it was important was not revealed. All that mattered was its utterance.

The Dwellers had created a whole mythology based upon this number. They never expected it to become real, and in their suspicion of all outsiders, were not sure what to make of the discovery of any traveler, let alone one, who knew the password. The Elders were interested in the nature and purpose of such outsiders. As it might on occasion be a trick to discover the whereabouts of their secret Forest home, they were extremely cautious and protective of such information.

After a long thoughtful silence, there came a calm determined response from the invisible Julian, "I call in the name of the Three. Will the Tribe of the Forest do as agreed?"

Thod shrugged to Quei and then replied to the bodiless voice. "We honor the words as promised long ago and welcome the friend of the Ones of the Palace as brother in our home."

"Yes, welcome. Now let's get out of here before whomever you are hiding from comes back!" Quei was uneasy talking to thin air. He wasn't sure what was really going on, just that whatever it was, it wasn't a game any longer. It seemed that this Julian, was indeed a Keeper of Legend. That was startling in itself, for a Keeper protected the Balance, a Balance that was clearly, by his appearance, in jeopardy. They would rush and present him to the Elders, especially to Buold.

Rmont was proud of himself for getting the full support of the Riders. Lord Merm would be relieved to know that everything was now underway. The search for the thief and the Key was just a matter of 'catching up', not one of discovery. Gorg, Tan and five others including Rmont were mounted and out of the Ice Barrens. They were headed for the Burning Forest! The writing on the box was leading them there. The hieroglyphics indicated that the Key was of the Old Ones and must be returned to Tika.

Tika was the proverbial origin of the Old Ones.

Specifically it was the territory to the northwest of the Burning Forest nestled in the canyons. It was a fabled city at the highest point of the worlds. It was well known to all, the fable was not concerned with its location, rather that it was once a great place of magic. Now it was nothing more than a crumbling ruin. It was no more than two sun risings away.

To approach the city Rmont and the Six would have to cross the uppermost tip of the Burning Forest along the Pass River and through the Falls of Light. It was then a steady hard climb up narrow winding paths through the canyons to the city that overlooked all. Rmont had never been all the way to the top, but had crossed the Falls of Light in a younger time. He had found it too treacherous to continue far along the carved out ledges of the canyons and only could view the lofty ruins from a distance. He had always wished he had been able to complete that pilgrimage and now excitedly anticipated this venture. All rode not speaking, with Rmont at the lead. The Sun was now high in the sky. Pictures of glory and success ran through each of their minds.

There had been no time to inform Lord Merm of the successful commencing of the pursuit. Rmont believed that Merm would realize that the seven were under way after he hadn't returned, or the Riders hadn't sent back a piece of his ugly body for ransom! Besides, the Lord Merm never imagined any other outcome. All these ideas ran through Rmont's head. He inhaled a deep breath of the fresh Barren air. In the distance he could just begin to make out the edge of the Burning Forest.

The Burning Forest! A chill ran through him. Gotts were not afraid of anything, but the Forest provided an unknown adversary. He was well acquainted with all the horror stories of those who were lucky enough to find their way back out of the mysterious Forest after entering. Whenever possible, ingress was avoided. It was more prudent to take the longer way around in order to reach a destination. In this instance, only the most minimal entry would be made and in bright sunlight. They would be in the Forest for half a sun rising. Even that would be long enough to court the dangers of whatever it was that lurked in and protected the Forest!

It was said amongst the Gotts, that creatures who ate the flesh of travelers, lived there. They never revealed themselves or confronted any intruder. They just followed and waited and then without any warning or alarm, members of the party accessing the Forest, one by one, without a noise, vanished, never to be heard from again, except in one or two rare cases. No-one had ever seen any of these creatures, but the stories of their cannibal brutality spread throughout the worlds. It was so frightening that the Burning Forest was left alone and not traveled in under normal circumstances. These were not normal circumstances. A brief crossing would be made in order to cut the time for reaching the city of Tika.

The Riders also had knowledge of the stories, but they would never openly admit to any type of reservation in passing through the Forest. Gorg's usual excuse was that there was no profit to be found there, so why bother! As the most direct route to Tika was to go into the upper North west corner, and as time was of the essence in order to find the thief, it was accepted with all its inherent risks. Gorg sped up and came next to Rmont. "We rest now short while, soon closer be to Forest. Not wise stop there," he pointed to the Forest, and the distant smoke filled air, " reach other side then okay."

"Agreed. I don't wish to stop for any reason, once inside that place. Do your Six understand the plan?"

"Yes. Fastest way is. Much trouble there is."

"Then gather your Six and we will stop here for a short rest. Tell them to eat and drink now. We will

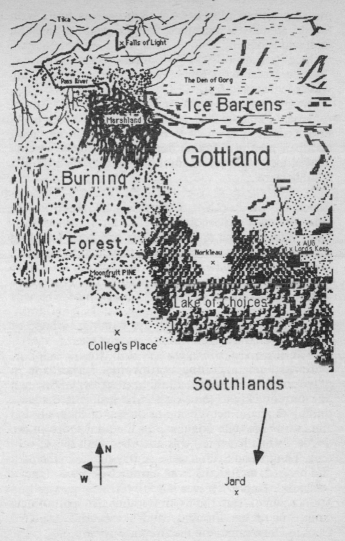

'Tika' Map of the Northlands

not stop within the Forest." Rmont was gruff with Gorg. It was the accepted way of dealing between Gott and Rider.

Gorg took no offense. He turned back to his Six. "We here rest short time. Eat, drink. Journey long will be when next rest."

The Six gathered together and dismounted. Rmont remained separate and alone. The trip through the Forest ahead was about to begin. It would certainly test their mettle! Though none mentioned their trepidation, they all were intuitively aware of each other's apprehension.

Deep to the South in Jard, Darla had been awake since the early dew moistened the start of a new sunrise. While Rmont and the Riders had been traveling toward the Burning Forest, she had been anxiously expecting Thiunn and Eruinn. Why were they so late?! She became agitated with their tardiness and the worry about...something...she wasn't clear what. She was starting to feel an urgency. She paced back and forth, occasionally peering through the window in hope of seeing the arrival of the young Chosen Ones.

Ever since the confrontation with the *Evil* force, Darla had felt a pulling northward. Julian was in grave danger and needed all three right away. She had to return quickly to the North. She just sensed something like a cold net closing in on top of them all and Julian was not fully cognizant of the total scope of the threat. While her mind was absorbed with these feelings, Thiunn and Eruinn came scurrying down the path and banged through the front entrance of the cottage.

"Darla! Darla!" It was hard to tell who was calling out her name, from the room within. Gradually Darla came out of her thoughts and as she did, the two Chosen Ones came into the fireplace room.

"Darla! She's not there! We couldn't find her anywhere. Even the neighbors were gone!" Thiunn was flustered.

"Where have you been?" Darla only half heard his words. She vented her frustration of waiting for them to return, "I was just about to leave without you! We don't have the time to waste," she noticed a frown on their faces and suddenly heard what had been said to her by Thiunn, "She's gone? What are you talking about?"

"Mother! The cottage is empty and she's nowhere to be found!" Eruinn was irritated by the slowness of Darla to comprehend.

"Settle down you two. There has to be a good reason. She probably went to visit friends."

"But who? Where? There is no note. That isn't like her," Thiunn continued.

"We can't wait to find out. We must go back to the North. Your Uncle is in trouble."

"But what about Mother? What if something is wrong?" Eruinn spoke in a pleading tone.

"Don't worry so much. She is safe. We have a job to finish and must go now."

"How do you know where Uncle J is? Eruinn and I haven't a clue."

"I am sensing a very old threat. Your Uncle is still in the North. He has the Key and others are almost upon him, the same ones as we encountered here."

"Here?" Eruinn recalled the sight of his brother and the blue opaqueness that had almost overpowered him in this very room. "Haven't we done enough. Why do we have to go on?"

At that moment of his asking and without warning Jewel began to glow. Then, as before, a high pitched melody was faintly evident. All three became afraid that it was the return of the same entity as before, but it wasn't. Darla also started to glow and then, like the first time when they had met in the garden, a strange ominous voice that was Darla's, but not Darla's, emanated from her mouth.

"Chosen Ones! Do not squander what is left," the voice was friendly but firm, "Your task is not yet complete. You must continue and hurry to the ancient place."

Eruinn broke from his amazement. "Who are you? How do you know all these things?"

"Young one, we are of before and what is to be. We are many like you. You are shared with us."

"What do you mean? I don't understand." Eruinn was pleasant.

"We were the voice in the water. The voice of those that have gone before. We are here to help but cannot. We are here to share and guide, but we do not lead. It is you who must act. You are of the Chosen. The tests have been passed."

Thiunn who had been watching and listening broke in. "But why us and what are we meant to do. We are just..."

"You are the Chosen Ones. There is much to learn. There is great magic for the Balance. You must help the Stoneman who is now a Keeper of the Three. The Balance is unsettled. You must help to protect it. There is the Light and the Dark. The Dark now seeks the Magic. It will change the Balance. The Dark must be stopped by the Light. You are Chosen and part of the Light. The other parts require your strength to re-establish the Balance."

"But what is all this light and dark and balance?" Thiunn was bewildered.

"There is not enough time to explain all, we cannot remain dominant too long in any of you," the voice obviously meant their use and speaking via Darla, "but we will tell you of some. We are all part of the worlds. Long ago we each lived as you do now. We were part of the Chosen to guard the Balance of the worlds. There was long harmony, but when needed, we would protect all from those who would disturb the Balance." It wasn't clear if the plural meant many individuals, or many within one individual, "Those who presently disturb were once part of the Balance, but now have been enticed to serve another. They, in their desire for more power, seek to use that part of the Light and will darken the world forever. The wisdom of this is now held by a Keeper. He must secure this wisdom against the *Evil* ones." Darla was weakening, which caused the voice to pay note to its priorities, "We have not got long. You must all go to the place of the ancients. There you will know what to do. Beware! The Darkness is strong and knows of your coming," the voice's tone had more urgency in it, "There is little time. Even now..." The voice faded, Jewel stopped glowing and Darla collapsed. Thiunn rushed forward in an attempt to break her fall. Eruinn remained where he was trying to put all of this into some meaningfulness.

Within a few moments Darla was coming back to normal consciousness. Thiunn hovered over her and as she opened her eyes he smiled a big grin at her. "Well. What was that you were saying about no time to waste! Are you alright?"

"Yes," she was a bit groggy, "Yes I'm fine."

"That was quite a show you put on. It was the same voice as the first time it happened."

"An Old One?"

"Yeah. Don't you remember?"

"I can remember the sense of it but not the exact words. It was like I was sitting back and watching from a long distance."

"We had a chance to ask questions."

"Questions?"

"It told us about Uncle J. It said something about the light and dark magic, and *Evil* ones. We must protect Julian and the Balance, whatever that is, and go to the place of the ancients."

Darla remained quiet, then, after seeing Eruinn standing off to the side, asked: "What's up with him?" she indicated the other brother.

"Eruinn," there was no acknowledgment, "ERUINN!" Thiunn called louder and shook Eruinn verbally from his trance. "Come over here!" Eruinn stepped over to them, "What was that all about?" Thiunn meant that which resembled a daydreaming state. "Are you okay?"

"Yes, yes I'm fine. I was just trying to understand all that talk coming from Darla. Do you understand it?" He threw the question at Thiunn and Darla.

"It was a voice of the Old Ones," Darla searched her *knowing* as she spoke, "Not just one but many. It was their group consciousness, like the Magic. It lies deep within us, but cannot be too dominant. It is there for us to draw on, like a type of intuition. An intuition with much more accurateness and magic. Things must be critical for it to swell forth and speak." Darla was recalling her own limited understanding of the manner in which the Old Ones had placed themselves in selected families; always there and ready to act, but also dormant and unannounced till the time of need. She had been aware longer than Eruinn or Thiunn or Julian for that matter, but had only a little more comprehension of its purpose and use. She realized however, that it was a gift to be cherished and respected. "I believe we should move out of here and get to the place of the ancients."

"Where is that?" Eruinn asked in a tone that displayed his frustration with all that had happened. After all, hadn't the war with Merm and the Gotts been won! "I thought we would be able to remain here awhile longer. Perhaps find Mother?"

"The war with the Gotts was never the real *Evil*. There are others more threatening than Merm. Remember last night?!" Darla watched the reaction of the two, "This is the magic of the Dark that continues to pursue. They can't be far behind us, or your Uncle. We have to go, there isn't anyone else. WE are the Chosen. I told you at the beginning of our journey that there was no turning back once you started on the path of the Chosen. There is no choice. As for the place of the ancients, that is in the lost city of the Old Ones, Tika. In the north beyond the Burning Forest."

"Well if it's lost, how are we going to find it?" Eruinn was sarcastic.

"The city is not lost. It just refers to the fact of its losing the glory of the ancients who lived there. It is now a pile of rubble on the canyon top, but once it was said to have been magnificent. The magnificence and the society that lived there are lost to future generations, not the place. We will travel through the western Forest to the Pass River and then on to the 'Falls of Light'. From there it is a tough climb up the old pathways through the mountains till we reach its top and, Tika. It will not be easy!"

"But is it safe to go into the Burning Forest! Isn't it full of terrible creatures?" Thiunn interjected, "I've heard all the stories of travelers wandering in and never coming out!"

"There is no other way. It is the fastest most direct route. We need to get there before the *Evil* arrives."

As they conversed, there was a whistling sound becoming audible from outside. It seemed to come from down the main path which led to Julian's cottage. All three stopped to listen. Thiunn went to the front room to have a look through the window, and returned in a flash.

"Its Sergeant Zer. He's coming this way!"

"Oh no. I think he was here last night. He didn't see me but he noticed the lit fire. He probably thinks that transients are squatting here and is keeping a check. There is no time to linger. It may already be too late! Grab whatever you can immediately find. We will leave through the back, just like our last journey. Quickly! We don't want him to find us. He would be required to keep us detained and that would make us lose valuable moments. Moments that might mean the difference of life or death later to us or to your Uncle. Now get to it!"

Sergeant Zer was on his way to his morning shift. He had decided last night to check in on Julian's cot-

tage in the morning, just in case the transients he sus-
pected last night had returned. He was casually
strolling along. As he neared the cottage, he thought
he heard a loud clanging noise. He picked up his pace
and began to visually scan Julian's property. When he
turned down the path which led onto the front garden,
he caught a glimpse through the corner of his eye of
something in the back, off to the side. It was moving.
He yelled out: "Hey you, stop!" He raced to the side
gate, and fumbled with the latch, but it did not budge.
As he stood there frustrated by his inability to unlatch
the gate, he clearly saw off through the back corner of
the garden, leading into the thick undergrowth, three
figures carrying sacks. They were disappearing into
the protection of the leaves: "Hey YOU! STOP!" It
was too late. The thieving transients had escaped!

- - - - - - - - - - - - - - - - - -

After they had finished dinner, Lord Merm again
stressed the importance of Rmont connecting with the
Riders and recovering the Key. They both decided
that Rmont would leave immediately for the Ice
Barrens. He would arrive early in the next sun rising.

Merm now sat alone at his large work table studying
the third of the five Forbidden Books. This was the
book that spoke of the Key in the greatest detail. He
was searching for anything that could help secure it
safely and without incident He needed to know the
reason for the thieves returning to Tika, where the
box's (which was placed in front of him open on the
table) hieroglyphics indicated it must go if found.
What was there in Tika that drew the Key? As much
as he read, Merm could not find any reference to the
subject. There was all the history of the Old Ones
who had originally lived in that canyon top citadel; of
their great wealth and magic, but not one word on anything else. It was perplexing!

Merm was becoming weary of the fruitless search.

He had been through so much lately and found that he tired more easily. His eyes were heavy and he had to keep catching his attention from drifting off to restfulness. He reached a conclusion: it was time to turn in and get some sleep.

Putting down the book he rose and crossed the castle room to his bed. The fire felt warm as it crackled throughout the stone room. He turned down the light and lay on the top of the bedding. He would lie a moment before disrobing and climbing between the covers. There was so much that needed to be done. How was he going to get to Tika and meet with Rmont as planned? The authorities from the South were keeping a strict watch over him. How was he going to reclaim the Key and all the magic it would give? It seemed impossible that he would ever clear his thoughts enough to sleep. He was not alone. Dorluc was intervening. Dorluc was trying to calm Merm, to tire him, so that he would sleep and then be vulnerable to his *Evil* power.

Gradually Merm's mind went to restfulness, as he fell deeply to sleep.

Dorluc had been waiting for this moment. It had been a long wait since the last influencing. He would encourage Merm, now that he had discovered the thief in the Forest, to pursue and capture him from the Dwellers. It was the early morning and the view screen was tuned into the castle room. Merm lay asleep fully clothed upon his bed. Dorluc scanned the room. Upon the table were the books and there...there was the box that had held the Key! Dorluc smiled. This would be of help. He must act now. There would still be just enough time to enter Merm's dreams before his awakening. In fact, this was the best time of influencing, in the half consciousness from sleep to wakefulness.

Dorluc would need help in affecting Merm. He summoned the others who were banished with him. When they all arrived around the view screen he gave the instructions:

"Direct your energy to me. We will link as one." As he spoke he held out his hands, one to either side and took hold of a hand of each of those next to him. The rest copied till all were linked physically together, "and then I will enter Merm's dream. We will direct him to the thief in the Forest and reveal our ability. Begin your transference."

One by one, each around the screen closed their eyes and concentrated toward Dorluc. It was time to invade Merm's thoughts! Dorluc hesitated slightly while he considered the gravity of the event. This was his opportunity to redeem himself in the eyes of Wakan. He still needed to keep Wakan happy with their alliance. Wakan had knowledge that would be needed to escape this spiritual place once the Key unlocked the *Passwords*.

Wakan, like Dorluc, was of the Old Ones, but with greater control and abilities within the Magic. The Old Ones had a hierarchical order which was based upon knowledge of the Magic. There were various tiers of awareness of the Magic and the Balance. Each tier had its own responsibilities toward discovery and maintaining of the Balance of this Magic throughout the various worlds that comprised their firmament. Wakan was of the second tier, and Dorluc the seventh. There were seven tiers in all. The seventh tier was the least skilled in the Magic. The inner grouping of the first tier were known as the 'Ydnew'. The Ydnew had the greatest knowledge and ability within the Magic and therefore became the leaders amongst the Old Ones in their ancient city of Tika. There was never much need to police their community, as all of the seven tiers had self governing as part of their mandate. To be in violation of any of the missions of the tiers was inconceivable! It was savage, and not believed to be a part of the hybridized society of the Old Ones.

Many eons ago the Old Ones had been like the other gatherings of the world, but now they were evolved beyond such primitive existences. They spent their time in peace and harmony. Their main job was to protect the Balance and allow the other gatherings to peacefully evolve without undue influence.

The Balance was a powerful force of the worlds; a connective medium, an anchor that kept them all in order and place. If the medium became stretched or broken, absolute chaos would reign and the *Evil* side of the Balance prevail. The *Evil* side was the force of all that is negative in the worlds. It would devour and corrupt whomever it could, if it was not kept in constant check by the *positive* side. The Ydnew directed the tiers of their society to maintain that crucial Balance. The slightest tampering could force a sudden swing to the *Evil*, causing irreparable destruction.

Just as the *Evil* had immense power, so did the *positive* side. It would allow a happy productive existence that would eventually lead those who practiced that Magic to pass through stages of development, like the Old Ones had, till they would eventually go on to the next level. Because of initially Dorluc's, then Wakan's *Evil* tamperings, all became imprisoned at their own tier. All of these levels of existence were intricately bound to each other. Each required the other to be moving within a positive Magic, so that they could continue on to their own respective paths unhindered. The meaning of life in any of these levels was to meet and solve these challenges. Movement to the next level was dependent upon leaving behind a safer Balance within that level. It was therefore in the interest of the Old Ones to leave behind a safer place, so that they could freely and speedily move through their next challenges!

When Dorluc had been caught trying to access the Magic for his own *Evil* ends, and sequestered all those ages ago, there had been many questions. It was believed that he must have had an accomplice or accomplices other than his fellow seventh tier followers. He had used skills and knowledge far beyond his seventh tier which were not yet available to him. Though Dorluc had been allowed greater access to the knowledge than most of the Old Ones of the seventh tier, he had displayed awareness of power and secrets that would have, for others, required more informed assistance. He must have had help from within the Ydnew or second tier! It was believed that one amongst them was involved, but it could never be proven.

After Dorluc's involvement was substantiated and he was given his punishment, the whole issue was quickly forgotten. Dorluc would never again be a bother, or so they thought. He was banished to the Land of No Form, and it was believed that the threat to the Balance was gone with him there. He was stripped of his corporeal existence and locked safely away, trapped in the Land of No Form.

The Land of No Form was a timeless, vague, spiritual realm, apart from the rest of the firmament. He would never be able to return to Tika or continue on after the Old Ones to the next tier. This tier was not the elysium of the other gatherings' philosophies. It was the next step of graduation that all creatures eventually rise to, once complete knowledge of the corporeal universe had been discovered and understood. In time, all gatherings would reach it. It was not death, but rather a releasing of the spirit from its physical limitations.

Ages had passed and eventually the Old Ones, tier by tier left this world, starting with the second tier, till a void existed. They had gladly left behind all limitations of their bodies. Before his turn to leave his worldly existence, one Old One secretly created a means by which Dorluc could acquire more magic from within his banishment and eventually find a means of escape! That Old One was Wakan. He did not completely 'go on' with the others. Instead he created a portal through which he could momentarily slide between the tiers of existence. It would not be easily detected, and it would not alter the Balance until it was too late for anyone to stop him from his intended purpose.

Wakan was superior to Dorluc in skill and magic. He, like the others had understood great mysteries and Magic. Unlike the others, he used the power for his own personal gain. Wakan had been corrupted by the *Evil* side of the Balance. He wanted more power, more control. He would only be satisfied with his domination of the Worlds!

Wakan needed Dorluc to help him from the Land of No Form to manipulate Merm in the physical world. He would help Merm to discover and then physically control the Key and *Passwords of Promise*. It was still possible for Dorluc to be released back into that world with the knowledge of Wakan and the power of the *Passwords*.

Wakan, however, was not now able to return to corporeal existence without the power of the Key and *Passwords* released. When the time had come, he had chosen to 'go on' with the others; there had been no other option. To refuse would have drawn suspicion and perhaps reopened the issue of Dorluc and his undiscovered accomplice. As a result, Wakan required some ally with knowledge of magic to assist in acquiring the instruments of the Key, as he was only able to communicate for very short moments in this world without drawing the attention of the Old Ones. He needed someone to find the Key that would unlock the *Passwords of Promise*. Dorluc was his only possibility. But there was a catch. The Key and The *Passwords* could only be manipulated by one of power who was in physical form. The Key required the touch of a corporeal being to begin the process of unlocking! As a result, in order to completely rekindle their spark of permanent existence within this physical world left behind by the Old Ones, and realize their wishes, they both needed to join with each other to influence someone to their cause. It had taken many attempts to find a suitable pawn. They had failed once before with Ho, but now with Merm, felt victory near. Merm would ignite the process of the 'unlocking' and then hand it over to Dorluc and Wakan. From that point on there would be no stopping their incarnations!

The joining of Dorluc and Wakan had developed out of necessity and was not a happy alliance. Both privately vowed that when they possessed the secrets of power and magic that the *Passwords* contained, there would be no more need to tolerate one another; treacherously their alliance would be ended! For now however, there was an unspoken understanding. Dorluc wanted the knowledge to find the Key and *Passwords* that only Wakan could supply, which would release him from his imprisonment. Wakan wanted the power of the *Passwords* that he could only access through Dorluc by way of Merm. All of this had to be accomplished without setting off alarm. It was very intricate. To add to the complications, the Old Ones though they had moved on, were not dead. They could still protect that which was left behind using precautionary measures, which had been left on standby in case a threat to the Balance occurred. This was accomplished by burying deep within members of the worlds great knowledge and magic. During times of threat these inner moles would surface and deal with the threat. They would have power beyond their tiers, and access to the Magic. If these preliminary measures were not adequate to deal with the problems, then there were a series of other more powerful moles who would awaken. Finally, if those did not manage to defeat the dangers, then the Old Ones themselves would be alerted and come to return the Balance. The Balance had to be maintained and the Magic protected. It was the greatest magic of all! A Magic that would give unsurpassable strength and domination. It could not be allowed to fall to *Evil* control; a control that both Wakan and Dorluc desperately sought after. They believed that once the wisdom was theirs, they would be omnipotent! But first Dorluc must complete his part and acquire control of the Key. To this end Merm was invaluable.

Gradually Merm's tired mind changed under the Evil's influence. The blankness of fatigue was being replaced by images of another place. Merm was standing alone. It was foggy. There was no warmth, light, nor fear. Just a sense of a presence. He questioned in his half subconscious dream, *"Who is there?"* He stood still listening in his dream for a sound. Again, *"Who is here with me? Why am I in this place?"*

"Do not be afraid. I am a friend," Dorluc's language felt familiar to Merm, "We have met before," again gradually as Merm listened in this half dream state, an image of Dorluc materialized two or three lengths away. It was opaque and shaky. "It is I who have been with you all this time, guiding and helping when the need was strong."

Merm recognized the voice, and began to remember the many dreams that had seemed so real and then come true since his rise to power. *"Why do you come to me now?"*

"I know where the Key that was stolen from you is, and I have come to help you to retrieve it before it falls into the wrong hands. It has great power and will enable he who controls it to dominate the worlds. That domination is meant to be by the Gotts. Others will misuse the great magic and harm us," Dorluc was playing his part well.

"Yes I know of these things. The Key was stolen from me. If it wasn't for the warning that awakened me, it would have been gone without a trace. I almost had the thief but she had the help of others..."

"It was I who tried to wake you in time," Dorluc interspersed this thought, "but I was too late. The Others kept me from warning you, allowing them the time to escape with the Key. You understand what we are up against?"

"Yes. But what can I do? I am watched constantly.

I cannot go anywhere without suspicion, yet I must go if I am to control the Magic of the Key before the Others you speak of do."

"There is a way. You must travel to the Burning Forest. It is there that the thief has run. He has solicited the aid of the Dwellers. He must be stopped before he can deliver the Key to the Others that I speak of. They are *Evil* and dangerous."

"How can I do this, I am always under observation?"

"There are many secrets in this castle room of which you are not aware. There is a passage out of this room and into tunnels which travel far below the surface."

"Yes. They are found, but I do not know my way through these. I would become lost and never find my way out!"

"I speak of another way. Do you not have the container of the Key?"

"Yes. It was left behind by the thieves."

"The container also provides minimal magic. If you hold your first three fingers of either hand against the writings in the lid of the box, you will not be visible to any of your world for as long as your fingers remain in contact with the hieroglyphics. You will be heard and smelt, but not seen. Take the box and go to the Burning Forest."

"But where?" His dream mind was very pliable. There was never any conflict or aggression in this state for any who were influenced. It was drug-like.

"South of the Pass River, west of the Marshlands in the northwest. Go there as fast as you can."

"How will I know where to find these Dwellers?"

"When you are near enough they will find you. When that occurs, use the magic of the box. After they give up on locating you, follow them back to the home of their tribe. It is the only way. There, if you hurry, you will find the thief and the Key."

"Who should go with me? I have sent Rmont to the Riders, to go to the city of Tika."

"Tika? Why Tika," had Dorluc missed something?

"The Forbidden Books are in a similar language to that within the box. Those hieroglyphics show it's origin is from there and to 'there' it must be returned. I noticed the meaning quite by mistake." Merm's voice was slurred by the dream state and the influence. He could not conceal the complete truth from the *Evil* in his answers, whether he wanted to or not. Dorluc, who had been strongly influencing Merm became cautious. This influencing of dreams created a tremendous drain upon the dreamer, and if pushed too far the 'victim' would never awaken from the dream state. This was part of the danger of influencing those outside of Dorluc's domain. Dorluc would hasten his visit.

"It is interesting, but the thief is in the Forest with the Dwellers. It is there you must go alone," Dorluc considered the possibility that the city of his ancestors might be the real destination. If the thief was permitted to travel to Tika, it would become extremely difficult to help or participate in any manner. It was the home from which he was eternally banned. All of his abilities were powerless there. He could only hope to retrieve the Magic of the *Passwords* before that eventuality. Merm must be encouraged to accomplish this mission without delay. "If the thief reaches Tika, all will be lost. You must find him and intercept him before that happens."

"I understand."

"One last thing," Dorluc had only moments left before Merm was too drained to awaken, "The other thieves are on their way. They have been given magic to help them. With the box you will be able to conceal yourself. Do not let any of them know of your presence. They can also lead you to the completion of your task, should something go wrong."

"Yes. I understand."

With that Merm was suddenly aware of only his own presence. He was asleep, but he wondered at the realism of the dream. When he awoke, he would gather together those things he would require and using the magic of the box, walk out of the castle and Norkleau enroute to the Burning Forest.

- - - - - - - - - - - - - - - - -

In the view screen room where Dorluc and his followers still stood linked together physically and mentally, Dorluc opened his eyes. One by one each link in this chain released one another.

"Do you believe he will accomplish the task?" One follower asked, "What of the mention of Tika?"

Dorluc considered all the words exchanged with Merm before replying. "There has been much awakening in the past while. Things that we long ago thought were gone are still among us. Those that sent us here have placed much magic and planning in protecting the Balance of the worlds. This was all unknown to us, and has been carefully worked out. Now that it is obviously triggered we will have to proceed cautiously. It will not be a simple task, but we are more prepared than most to deal with these handicaps. Those that are just awakening are not practiced in their magic. There is still time to take advantage of them in their naive period of discovery. It will be a matter of which group is quickest and shrewdest at applying these new found abilities."

"But what if they manage to enter the zone of Tika? What can we do then?" another questioned.

"We cannot allow that to happen. It will remove any influence we now have. We will be unable to predict the outcome if any other than us discover the true purpose and Magic of the Key and *Passwords*. The others cannot return, but if the Magic is released prematurely, then there will be a mightier foe with whom we will have to contend. It is better to avoid that outcome. Tika is a long way off. They will have alot to cope with before they are able to enter that

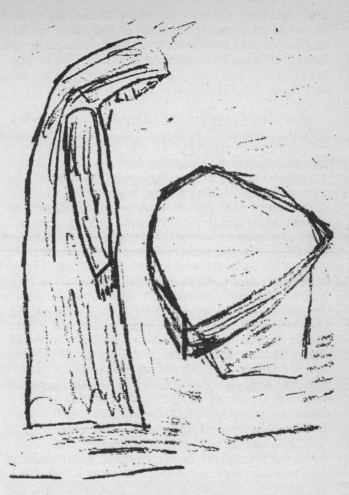

Dorluc and the View Screen

zone. It will be up to all of you to set the traps necessary to slow down any move in the direction of Tika.
Now go, there is much to do!"

One by one they left the tiny dim room. Dorluc

gazed into the view screen to watch the images being presented as possible sources to the drain in the Magic. He was comfortable with the influencing of Merm, believing that the effect would be long lasting and prevent Merm's own greed from usurping the direction of his *Evil* and seeking after the Magic for himself.

Everything was beginning to work smoothly again, since the disaster of Merm with the South and the unexpected loss of the Key. Dorluc still worried about the cunning way in which his forbearers had seeded protection for the Balance throughout the worlds. He was not certain what, if any, unpredicted surprise would rear its head just at the moment when complete success was at hand! He had waited so long, even before Ho, to regain his corporeal being and present himself to the weak and unsuspecting real worlds. Nothing would be allowed to get in his way. Not even the left over tricks of his compatriots!

He mulled over contacting Wakan, to ask for some assistance. No, he would wait. Even Wakan would have to be dealt with at the appropriate time. Too much information given to this transitory ally would only make more difficult the process required to sever their association; one that presently served both parties well. In Dorluc's view, Wakan was old and impotent, but he still knew of things that Dorluc did not. He would no longer need this knowledgeable master, once the Key and *Passwords* were under his domain.

He grinned confidently as he glared into the screen, not seeing the images presented there, but imagining the ones of mastery in his own thoughts. It would not be long now. After all those times and attempts to re-establish himself in a world that had, in his mind, been cruel and unkind in its punishments towards him, everything was finally coming to fruition!

Chapter 6.

It was the middle of the sun rising. Jard was now far behind the three. Their exit from the cottage and Zer had been close, but no-one had followed after, and they were well on their way.

They followed a similar route as the first trek northward. This time the only difference was that they would be traveling just west of Colleg's place and into the Burning Forest by way of the Moonfruit Pine. All were unaware of the name of the wood of that place, and it's magic! The pathways were quiet, as not much of the commerce of the area had returned to normal hours of operation.

The air was fresh, and the land undulating. The undergrowth of newer wood was full of green and still a little damp from the early rain that fell in these parts at that time of year. A rain that from the appearance of the clouds overhead, was about to fall again soon. The images that were born of such natural tranquillity, were soothing to their weariness from travel. They marched on in silence as droplets of water began to sprinkle.

"Maybe we should stop and wait the rain out?" Thiunn didn't like the idea of becoming soaked, "Its going to pour soon!"

Darla reflected a moment on the surroundings, then: "The woods are always a little wet at this time. We'll survive as long as it doesn't really get heavy. Let's keep on going till it really comes down, we can stop in a while if we have to, but it would be good to reach the Forest before dark."

On they went. The sky was becoming more overcast, and the drizzle more constant. Still they did not stop. Up and down the path carried them onward. They soon were at the same northwestern level as Colleg's and not far from the beginnings of the Forest.

- - - - - - - - - - - - - - - - - -

By mid sun rise of the same day, away to the northeast, another had started a journey towards the Forest. Lord Merm was traveling north from Norkleau along the highest edge of the Lake of Choices. He would enter the Forest at its eastern side and then continue west until encountering *those* who lived in the Forest.

He had not been seen by any who he passed while leaving Norkleau, though he felt as if the Gotts he passed had looked right at him and identified him. For some reason they had not acknowledged his presence. The only proof that they hadn't actually seen him, was confirmed in a couple of instances, when, if he hadn't jumped out of the way he would have been run over or walked straight into! It wasn't till he had cleared the city and was alone on the path to the north, that he eased his grip upon the box, thereby becoming visible once more. It was a difficult change to accept, since according to Merm's eyes there was no change. He had always remained visible to himself! Obviously the magic of the box had worked, but he had difficulty in accepting that it did.

This was a wonderful for Merm. To be able to walk alone unnoticed. It reminded him of his younger times before his rise to greatness! His normal fear of being vulnerable in such a circumstance was not present, as long as he had the magic of the box. His only concern was that he would be able to find the right direction to follow once in the Forest. He wondered at the success or failure of Rmont in his mission. Where might he be? Had the Riders agreed to help once again? There was no way of knowing. On he went, the sky became more overcast and he neared the end of the edge of the

Lake; soon he would be in the Forest!

- - - - - - - - - - - - - - - - ◄ - -

The Elders were sitting together in a circle on their meeting dais. This was the ceremony of the meeting. The sun had risen and they gathered to greet it and discuss the issues and events of the intrusion of this traveler, Julian, in their secluded existence. They felt that a great trouble was about to commence! Buold was first to offer the traditional greetings, which were followed by an answer from each elder:

"It is good to be alive."
"And with friends."
"And with friends."
"And with friends."
"And with friends."
"And with friends." Each had been spoken as a group, but not together in any particular or similar rhythm.

"With friends together, on such a sun rise," said the last.

"This rising brings many new changes. I have seen the one from afar. He spoke to me about the time ahead," Buold was poetic in his phraseology, "The traveler comes with the sign of the ones before. They have told me this. We," he indicated the tribe, "must help. Great darkness follows. It is an *Evil* not of the worlds."

As he continued he added a strange substance to the smoldering fire in their midst. It was like fine hair, which, once the small flame touched, flashed into a short tiny blaze. After each blaze, Buold had said each of his words. The substance was magical, coming from the times before and was said to provide, by it's sharp aroma, a way through the ethereal zone, opening a clarity of thought to another sphere. One of great magic. Buold was the only master of this ancient art. It's secret was passed on through Head Elder, from generation to generation.

"The traveler carries the Balance, and is of more, than even he is aware. Three on three are prepared." He paused allowing comment.

"Three on three?" The others were not understanding of the meaning.

"All of the Balance from all sides is now open. It is now exposed and must be protected by Three on three. The traveler is the first of three. Each must go to the city. The Keeper waits." Buold was not able to explain more, since he only saw and could describe the visions of the dream, but not the meaning, "We are not to be combative, just misdirect and slow any not of the three who follow. The one from before told me this. Each will know the name and face of friends." His explanation of the dream was not challenged, "The sign of Three will be shown." It was all very unusual and mysterious. Each of the Elders was aware of the notification from the Moonfruit of the entry of the traveler and expected his arrival this sun rising. Unlike Buold they were not aware of the link of this to the Magic of old and the Ones of the Palace. So much of this knowledge had been unseen for so long, that it was unbelievable it ever had really existed! It wasn't likely to be *really* happening now, but it was!

The mysteries of the Magic of the Old Ones were almost forgotten by most of the Worlds, including the Burning Forest. Only a few still realized its power and dormant existence. Since so many Chosen Ones had perished during the Separation Wars, there remained little evidence or experience of their influence. Buold was still linked to that source. Not by his choice, but by the long ago seeding of the Old Ones, of his progenitors.

There were many moles and places that had been left undisturbed. Places where the Magic had been practiced and secrets of the Old Ones lived. Tika was one of these places. Of these locations Buold carried knowledge. A knowledge deeply placed, it had been dormant till the recent disturbances. Buold had been awakening to this knowledge. It would be his job and that of the Dwellers to help the three in whatever need. It would not take long for Buold's awareness to develop to the required level in order to be of most help. Though it was not fully appreciated, the Tribe was an integral part of the plans, made by the Old Ones, to protect the Balance if there ever was a menace.

"What can we expect upon the arrival of this traveler?" an Elder asked.

"More will follow of Light and Dark. We will have to use all our skill to see the danger. I will prepare for the traveler. The three must go to the falls and cross through its walls unto the pass under the canyons."

"Those ways have not been used since the Ones of the Palace! How will they know where to go?" another questioned.

"In the canyons there will be a way, but these things are only for the ears of the traveler. It will be up to the rest of us to keep watch for those of the Dark that follow. We will speak no more of this now, for eyes that cannot be seen wait and watch. We must send members of the tribe to survey our borders for more who come." Buold without realizing was speaking of Dorluc and his view screen and Merm, "All of these things are of the dream," this was a reference to the visions that he had, which were of the same source as the voice that had stopped Fon in the night from probing further into Julian. The mention of dream simply meant that, the Head Elder had acquired the information by way of a contact through the ancient Magic. It was accepted, though not completely understood by the others in the circle, but then that was why Buold was the Head Elder. Following a moment of pensive silence Buold stood and announced: "It begins."

The topic changed to other issues. This was the way of the Dwellers. Everything was taken in stride. They went on discussing other matters.

After all the Elders had spoken in turn on every and

any aspect of the circle of meeting; they finished with the simple words: "We have spoken enough. The time of asking nears!"

- - - - - - - - - - - - - - - - - -

Just past the mid point of the highest sun, the party of three arrived, though only two could be seen. Julian kept himself invisible in order to prevent Dorluc's early intervention. Quei and Thodox hurried down the wooded hill into the main path area of their tribe Dwelling place. Julian remarked how vacant it all appeared. His criticism went unchallenged.

"We will take you to Buold immediately. He is near." Thod got strange looks from the Dwellers who Julian had not yet grasped, were watching Quei and Thodox from their tree top homes and wondering who they were speaking to! The urgency of this delivery prevented stopping to explain.

Quei added: "Buold will be able to help you. He will know what to do."

"I hope there is a way to obstruct those that search for me. I do not wish to cause harm to any who live here. I will soon have to stop this little trick, and then it will only be a matter of 'when' they follow here, not if." Julian was growing tired by all the pressures lately placed upon him.

They continued down the path toward one large tree trunk. This was the home of Buold. There was no need for Quei or Thodox to call up to their Elder, even though they did, as their approach had been reported by the new sentries placed on the paths to the dwellings. As the two visible Dwellers stretched their vision upward, Buold walked out unto the balustrade which when built blended right into the branches of the tree.

"Only two of you? What happened to the traveler?"

"He is here," called out Quei, "beside us."

"What game do you play? I see no one beside you."

"We must come up. We will explain." Thodox was urgent in his tone.

"I will send down the lift."

The lift was made of wood. A series of pulleys and vines were ingeniously used to provide a lifting and lowering service to the tree tops. After a noiseless lowering, the ground party got into the lift. To Buold's inspection there were only two inside and they were keeping a good space between them. When they reached the top, Buold stood, his arms placed upon his hips and with a scowling face said, "So where is this traveler?"

"I am here," as Julian answered he gradually became visible.

Buold was taken aback, partially by the sudden voice out of nothingness which sounded familiar, and partially due the shock of Julian's re-materialization. This was the same voice as the one of the dream!

"With friends together on such a sun rise," Julian offered the sentence without prompting, something inside just blurted it out. He was now fully perceptible.

"And with friends," replied Buold with a grin of satisfaction. This was indeed one of the three, "Please come inside."

They all moved from the uneven landing and into the tree house. Julian marveled at its construction. Woven amongst the thick branches and with a thatched roof carefully camouflaged to resemble a green leafy tree, was hidden a large comfortable home. There was an entrance and a main room lushly decorated in the style of the Forest. All the chairs and tables were made from the Forest. There were windows on all walls providing magnificent views of the world outside. Off to one side was a kitchen where someone unknown to Julian, was preparing what was probably refreshment. To another side was a door beyond which Julian assumed were the sleeping quarters. Julian felt safe and warm.

"That is my mate," Buold indicated the Dweller in

The Pass River, Canyons and the Sign

the kitchen, "You must want some food and drink after the long hike through the Forest." He turned his attention to Quei and Thodox, "Well done, to both of you. You have made record time on this return trip. Please have some refreshments and allow the traveler..."

"I am called Julian," he was interrupted.

"...Julian, and myself to talk awhile. We will rejoin you shortly." Quei and Thodox sat on large wooden chairs with woven sweet grass seats and backs. Buold escorted Julian across to a closed door, opened it, and ushered him into not a bedroom, but a comfortable study. After the door was shut, leaving the two alone together, Buold continued in a less formal manner: "This is more relaxing and private." Julian sat and Buold walked to the window speaking as he gazed into the Forest.

"I was told of your coming. Of what help can the Dwellers be?" There was a soft knock at the door. The latch lifted and in came Buold's mate. She carried a tray of food and drink. Without a word she placed it upon the table which was in front of Julian. She gave him a reverent look.

"Thank you Myran." Buold, noticing her gaze indicated that she should leave them alone. She returned to the door and left.

"She is very curious." There was a moment of universality in the nature of intimate comments and mannerisms that males make of females, as Buold spoke. He moved to the table and poured drink. Julian took it, as well as something to eat. He was famished and it showed by the desperation of his eating. Buold decided to continue, giving Julian a chance to swallow a mouthful or so, "You have had a long journey. You are safe here with us."

"Thank you Buold," Julian sensed an amazement, "don't be alarmed by my knowledge of your name. There are many strange occurrences that have happened recently. I am not certain even how I come to know or say the things I am speaking. But what I say is true and in gratitude. I am fleeing from a great Darkness. It is imperative that I continue my purpose.

For I fear that my pursuers are near. I am sorry to bring them to your home, but they will come in search of me. I am not sure which way to go in order to escape their grasp?!" Julian was tired.

"Perhaps we of the Forest can provide some direction."

"I hope so. I was forced to leave three behind in order to get this far, and being alone without their council has been difficult."

Buold questioned, " three?"

"Those who started this journey with me. It was not safe to remain with them. The Darkness would harm them."

"You must not be concerned with what dangers befall others. We are all in this together and must do whatever part is written. I also have sensed things. There is a change amongst many," he meant himself, but would not reveal this directly. "What help do you need of the Dwellers?"

"I am not sure. I am looking for a sign of direction."

"There are no such things here. This is just a simple home. You speak of things long past and forgotten by most, as it should be. The Keepers of that knowledge were once to the north, in the canyons, but that is from our myth, no-one has traveled there since the times of Tika."

"How will I find my way to this Tika?" Julian picked up on the mention of Keepers and realized this was one of the signs of his quest, "Where must I go?"

"It is along the Pass River north in the canyons. It is nothing but ruins, but there are secrets hidden below. For the ones of choosing there is a faster way. Only they will know the one that points the way. From there is found the passage to the secrets below. Only the Chosen shall pass. These are the words of before. These are thoughts that have been placed long ago within."

Julian was silent as he mulled over these things. The answer was self-evident, he must go to Tika and hide the Key and *Passwords*. Only there, would they be protected. Perhaps there he would escape the Darkness. "What is this sign?"

"I do not know. Only the Chosen know." Buold was not able to inform.

"Then I must go to this Tika. Can you provide me with supplies?"

"More," he rose and went to the door, opened it, and called Quei and Thodox in, "Please join us," turned back into the room and as the two entered said: "You two will guide Julian to the canyons and the paths toward Tika. Once upon the paths you will return here."

"Yes, we can do that," Quei, who always spoke out, answered, "but why no further?"

"That is a journey for him alone. There are other reasons you are not able to know and there will be need of you within the Forest." Buold was firm.

"Thank you all. In the dew of the next sun rise I will leave. There is no time to waste." Julian rose up to show his gratitude and took the hands of the three.

"There will be time then for a brief ceremony to welcome you to our home. Quei will prepare your supplies, and Thodox will show you to a place where you can freshen up and rest. At the sun setting we will gather."

"Yes. That would be very nice. Thank you."

They clasped each others hands together in a circle and shook. This was the shake of friends of the Tribe. It had not be used since the days of old. Each of the Dwellers was afraid of the suddenness of this reawakening and arrival of Julian. They were concerned about what would follow, but realized that it was beyond their control. The quiet solitude of their existence was about to change, and they sensed it. There was strong magic involved; a magic not fully understood by them except perhaps by their Elder, Buold, who himself had been feeling different and frightened by a duality of person beginning to develop within him. He trusted Julian, but not the outcome.

Julian was pleased to have company again. It reminded him of Darla, Thiunn and Eruinn. He prayed they were safe and wished they were with him now, he needed them on this leg of his journey. He went into a slight trance as he stood with the Dweller. He was with Darla, Thiunn and Eruinn, in his thoughts. They stood joined together for what seemed an eternity, linked through time. It was an unexplainable sensation. An energy was flowing amongst them. All this was at the tip of their awarenesses. It gradually grew, changing their energy and their awareness. They could not let go. They did not want to let go. Their minds began to become slightly intoxicated and spin, their shared consciousness taking second position to another more magical force. They could not speak, but communicated their mortal confusion through their eyes. Then a melody of several notes came out of the air, and they all collapsed unconscious to the floor, thereby breaking their physical contact!

- - - - - - - - - - - - - - - - - -

Darla, Thiunn and Eruinn had just stopped to rest when they noticed a chill and began to sense something. They were near to entering the Burning Forest.

"Look, look at Jewel!" Eruinn was pointing out the beginning of a glowing amidst the stones in its hilt, "what does it mean?"

"Darla. It is like before!" Thiunn added remembering the episode in the Palace beneath the Stars.

"There is a strengthening of the Magic as it illuminates the light within the stones. We are close to it's source. Jewel is sensitive to its gathering. That means your Uncle and the Key are still safe on their journey." This was happening at the same time as Julian and the Dwellers in the treetops were grasping each others hands and beginning their spinning. It was a linking of power.

"Then we are headed in the right direction and

should meet up with Uncle J soon?" Eruinn was pleased that finally they were more certain of the rightness of their choice of leaving Jard and trying to catch up with their Uncle.

"Yes. It would seem so. These are all signs of a growing within the Magic. Light is representative of its source and strength. There must be others awakening with the power within to join the cause and protect the Balance. It would seem that the Darkness of the *Evil* will be challenged after all!"

At this moment and at the same time as the melody had played in the home of Buold, Darla's sentence was interrupted by that same tune. All of them stood spellbound wondering what was to come next. Nothing did come. After it had all passed the only difference was that Jewel continued to softly glow. There was no explanation that Darla could guess at. They decided to hurry on into the Forest and hoped to choose the correct direction.

By the beginning of sun set they were at the entrance to the Burning Forest. There would be a long twilight so they crossed from the flat rocky terrain into the dark musty green of the Forest. It was the blue green of the Moonfruit!

"These are beautiful trees," noted Thiunn. "They seem to have a personality. It is as if they speak."

"I feel it too," Eruinn was also feeling fatigued, "It is so peaceful and relaxing."

They walked deeper into the midst of the Pine. With every step they became more and more relaxed. By the time the evening dusk had started they were well into the Pine and without knowing, falling faster and faster into the grasp of the Moonfruit. Soon they would stop and find shelter to sleep in preparation of the next sun rise's journey.

It was during the fall of the darkness of the dusk that Darla realized that Jewel's glow had intensified.

"That's strange," she drew the two young Jardians to

her side, "see how the light is brighter. We must be close to some source of Magic here, or maybe nearer to your Uncle."

"Perhaps Jewel is guiding us to the source." Eruinn offered the idea.

"Maybe, but the change is growing even as we stand still. There is something much closer. Are you sensing anything?"

"I feel a presence, an influence. Though I do not sense a threat. Just peacefulness."

"Me too," Thiunn hated to be left out. "It is like a sweetness, calming and soothing."

"I have also felt the same. Something is here. Some magic surrounds us."

"What should we do? Thiunn and I sense no danger?"

"That is what bothers me. Why this sudden sense of wellness and relaxation? What is soothing our thoughts?"

"Maybe we're just tired?"

"No Thiunn, there is something more. Let's find a spot to rest for the night. We will take turns sleeping, while one stays awake. Just in case this feeling turns into something else!"

"Okay. How about under that big old Pine there?" Thiunn was pointing out Fon, "We can keep a better watch on that higher ground and get better cover under its larger branches."

"Sure, but we should be careful here." Darla's guard was up. A voice was calling. Whose was it?

As they neared the great old Pine, Darla's inner voice became stronger. About ten lengths from the Pine, Darla stopped.

"What's wrong," asked the nephews.

There was no answer. Darla raised her arm and waved off the two to wait. They stopped also. Darla probed her thoughts, then spoke out loud.

"Who are you? Why do you harm us?" There was a long pause and still nothing. The nephews exchanged questioning stares to each other and shrugged. "I know you are there. Reveal yourself. I will allow no harm to befall these two Chosen. Speak." Another long pause then Fon answered:

"I am Fon. Why are you in the Forest? You are not of the Dwellers. Why have you dared to enter?"

"We are seeking another. He is lost from us. Has he come this way?" Darla was cautious. Not yet understanding why Fon was trying to influence them or in whose service it was acting. Fon also was cautious not knowing if these outworlders were the *Evil* pursuers of the other, the Stoneman.

"Another has passed."

"When was this?"

"Another has passed."

"We seek another of before and now again."

"Is the other of the old?"

"He is of the Stone, of the Old Ones. Safe passage is asked in the name of those before," Darla realized that Fon was being careful with them and would only respond kindly if it could be proven that they were also of the Chosen, "We *three* are of the same as the other. Did the Stoneman pass safely by?" Darla wasn't quite comfortable with talking out loud to the air, but knew it had to be done.

"The One from before has passed to the inner Forest. It is safe now. Do you also wish to go there?" Fon was accepting these new South worlders. The mention of the Old Ones and Three had helped.

"Can you show yourself to me," Darla wanted to know to whom she spoke.

"I am before you." Fon sensed that Darla was confused, "I am of the wood, the great Moonfruit of the Pine."

"The tree?"

"Yes. I am of the wood."

Darla surprised by this revelation asked, "How is it that we speak?"

"We sense each other. Only few have learned to do

115

so, but fewer are able to commune without the touch. That tells us of your nature. You are also from before. You hold great Magic of the Ones before!"

"Will you direct us to the other? There is much danger behind and we must find and help him before the Darkness arrives." Darla conveyed her sense, and Fon agreed to help.

"We will show you the way and announce your travel. For now, rest. Later I will awaken you and show the way." With that, their communing ceased. Fon would send word immediately along the Pine to inform the Dwellers of these new arrivals who were also of the Ones before.

While all of this had transpired Thiunn and Eruinn wondered to whom Darla was speaking, as they could not hear any other voice.

"Who were you speaking to?" asked Thiunn.

"We are amongst friends here. Your Uncle has passed by here, and they will help us to follow him after we have rested," Darla was brief in her reply.

"But who is it that will help? We can't see anyone," Eruinn didn't accept her answer.

"We are amongst very old creatures here. The trees are more than mere vegetation. They are also alive with thought."

"I didn't hear a thing!"

"Me neither."

"Perhaps my capabilities are slightly more attuned to their form of communication. In time you will grow in these abilities. Now we must rest and in the sunrise they will show us where to find your Uncle."

Darla moved to the under branches of the great Moonfruit and sat down. She leaned against the trunk and closed her eyes. There was no more discussion. Thiunn and Eruinn, given no other choice or explanation, followed suit. Influenced by the ardor of the journey and the power of the Moonfruit all three were asleep in moments. It would be a peaceful sleep without any more dominance of the Pine. When they naturally awoke, Fon would indicate to them the correct destination. They would be met by the Dwellers before they got very far from the Pine.

- - - - - - - - - - - - - - - - - -

Merm also entered the Burning Forest at dusk. He crossed from the Gottlands' western most border. He was not used to such travel and knew he had gone as far as he could on this first sun rise. The walk into the Forest had been easier than he had expected. Nothing had trapped or captured him for dinner. The farther into the Forest he went the more confident he became that he would be able to handle any eventuality. He was beginning to enjoy being out in the wild on his own.

The Forest was heavy with vines and trunks of trees, trees that rose so high it was not possible to see their tops. The ground underfoot was uneven and unpredictable, forcing Merm to pay close attention to the placement of his steps. There was an eerie beauty untouched by the outside. There was not one sound. That was the most unusual aspect of being here. Merm expected to hear the loud variety of noises that should emanate, especially at the dusk, from such an old place.

Since beginning this trip, Merm had alot of time to think on his successes and failures. He tried to reach the fullness of certainty he had known before his rise. He laughed when he caught himself deep in such brooding. This was a sign of old age in his estimation. He was pleased to have been given this chance to be alone, but also wanted to put an end to the whole situation of the Key. How his desires had grown. No longer would the simple pleasure of ruling the Gotts satisfy. It was an addiction. He wanted more!

It was difficult determining in which direction he had traveled. The deeper into the Forest he went, the more difficult it was to get any bearing from the sky above. It was almost totally obscured by the growth of green of the trees. The idea that he might be lost dug away at him and his heart was racing. He didn't even know which way was out. Trying to calm his fear he kept moving in hopes to eventually come upon some proof of life. He would rather be caught by the creatures of the Forest and have company than remain alone and lost.

He began to whistle and occasionally sing a phrase or so of popular Gott songs. He no longer cared if it gave him away. He wanted to attract some attention, any attention!

"Down the path to the village below,
(Whistling in place of words to the rhythm of the words)
We all will see each other there,
Resting the dust of the path.
(Whistling in place of words to the rhythm of the words)
(Whistling in place of words to the rhythm of the words)
And bring us another round,"
(Whistling in place of words to the rhythm of the words)

It made no sense to the outside listener. It did however help to relax Merm. The echo of his voice and whistle made him feel in the company of his Troops.

The dusk changed to night. The darkness of the forest became intense. Merm had to stop. He surveyed the neighboring trees and shrubs, concluding that he would build a small fire to keep warm and sleep on the ground just over to the side in an area that was enclosed by vines and a fallen tree. He was protected from three sides. This would do fine. Gathering some pieces of vine near to him he made a fire. It was warm and comforting. He pulled his outer cloak over his body, lay back and drifted into sleep.

Dorluc was waiting. He still needed to influence Merm, to keep him on the track of the thief and prepare him for any dangers that might get in the way. It would be a short meeting. He would wait till Merm had fallen into a deep slumber. As he waited he continued his scanning of the worlds. He did not comprehend why the view screen had lost the image of the thief in the Forest with the Dwellers. Dorluc was relieved to see that Merm had managed so far on his first sun rise of travel. There was still time to catch up to the thief and the Key. Dorluc knew it was with that one. He could feel it! The view screen flicked from scene to scene, all of which were in the Forest, but it was dark and impossible to make out any detail. It flicked again, and this time found the now visible Julian! He was in the Forest with the Dwellers; in their encampment partaking in some sort of celebration! But where in the Forest? Dorluc had no clue. A new urgency to enter Merm's dreams arose. He could not wait. It must be done now!

Merm tossed as Dorluc created the proper state within the dream. Again Merm dreamt and saw himself standing alone in a mist. A voice, followed by the opaque blue form of a figure, was before him.

"The thief is in the Forest. He is with the Dwellers. You must find him before he leaves." Dorluc was direct.

"Where will I go? I do not know the way?" Merm was talking in a semi dream drugged state unable to resist and wanting the company and support.

"In the sun rise continue into the Forest. It does not matter where. Soon, those of the Forest will find you. Remember your magic and when they discover you, use it to learn more of the location of their secret home in the Forest. Follow them to the thief! You must hurry! I will try to help where I can. Now rest. Our trip is almost at an end. We will soon reclaim our rightful domain!"

The image in the dream vanished and Merm fell back into sleep. Dorluc would try to lead the Dwellers to discover Merm and they would hopefully, after losing their prisoner send a return messenger to warn their home. Then Merm could follow and the Key would be his again! Everything was going so smoothly. The Dwellers would be caught unaware, and then it would be too late for anyone to prevent the inevitable!

Chapter 7.

Quei with Thodox were debriefed much more thoroughly after Julian was shown to another tree top home to repose and refresh himself before the festivities of the evening meal. Julian found it interesting how the various tree top homes were interconnected through a series of vine tied sticks with one vine on either side acting as a rail to help steady the user from the bouncing of the 'vine walk'. Everything blended in so well, it was hard to tell which was natural and which was Dweller made. The scene was a perfect natural blend of nature and construction.

First Quei, then Thodox, retold every detail of the discovery of the traveler Julian, including the extraordinary behavior in the Forest, which led to his invisibility. Buold was intrigued. Clearly this Julian was much more than he 'appeared'. It was clear that the Dwellers would help him as they could, and the sooner he continued on his trip the better for all of them. After their debriefing, Buold then instructed them on what they both were to do in order to help Julian.

The lost city of Tika was known to all the Dwellers. What was not known, was the scope of the secret passages, which led from the north end of the Burning Forest along the Pass River to the hidden parts of that city. They made up a tremendous labyrinth. If the wrong one was taken, the traveler would be lost, and eventually perish without ever finding a way out. Buold was privy to the location of one of these passages and also the stories of the still concealed treasures that lay beneath its ruins. If it was not such a treacherous voyage to make, many more would have risked the passage to hunt for the truth of the legends. None had, and so the legends remained untested, but Buold knew of the one passage. He explained it's position to the two Dwellers, so that they could lead Julian to the correct spot. He would not give the exact location even to them, for according to the lore, any of the 'Ones' to come this way, would know the sign that would unlock the door to the correct and safe passage.

"You will go north past the western edge of the Marshland until you reach the mouth of the Pass River," Buold stressed, "From there you will follow the river against its flow through the Forest till it bends sharply to the mountains. There is a place there to cross. You will need strong arms to carry you across. The river is fast and deep, if you falter, you will be lost to its power. Once across, travel north through the trees and rocks until you reach the beginning of the mountains and again the Pass River running in the deep canyons. Here will be the sign and here you will leave the traveler Julian. From there he will know the way."

"How long will this take till we reach the mountain canyons?" Thodox wanted to have an idea of how to measure their progress once they started the trek north.

"It is a full sun rise from here," Buold hesitated, "You must not enter the passages with Julian. No matter what happens. Only the Ones of the Old may pass."

There was no more to be said. Buold dismissed them after again thanking them for their sacrifices. They would rejoin him, at the sun's setting with Julian at the festivities.

Quei knocked, the door unlatched and Julian, looking more rested and clean, welcomed him in. It had been a pleasant rest after the debriefing with Buold. Quei had had a chance to relax and refresh himself.

"Quei. Come In. I was getting worried that I had

been forgotten. This is a beautiful home." Julian was also relaxed and enjoying this place. It reminded him of his youth, and playing in the tree forts with his childhood friends in Jard.

"We are expected at the meal and should not delay long," Quei informed. He was wearing a fresh set of clothing.

"I'll be right along. I just want to get a couple of things." Julian meant the *Passwords*. They could not be left alone. As Quei entered and stood by the door Julian picked up the small red leather bound books and tucked them into the inside pocket of his coat, they would be safe there. Quei, who noticed, felt insulted that this Julian did not trust the Dwellers, but realized that he too would have done the same thing if the situation was reversed. "Thank you for waiting. Let's go!" Julian was almost his old jovial self!

They closed the door and proceeded to walk along the walkways that linked a few of the tree top homes. These few homes that Julian was amongst, were used as the official places and the center of any indoor festive activities. Julian found it hard to believe that these houses were so high from the ground below. It would be impossible for any passerby to see or hear their living above! The skill required to construct these places was very advanced.

As they made their way to the proper place along the vine walkway, they passed one home that was brightly lit with some sort of bulb acting like a spotlight. Then down a spiral walkway to another. Julian could hear the sound of others inside. Quei led the way, and opened the door of this one and with Julian close behind, stepped into a room filled with Dwellers. The Dwellers inside all grew silent upon noticing the arrival of the traveler. Buold stepped forward out of the crowd, and greeted Julian.

"Welcome friend to our meal. Join us as one." He guided Julian away from Quei and into the room to introduce him, eventually sitting him at a large table at

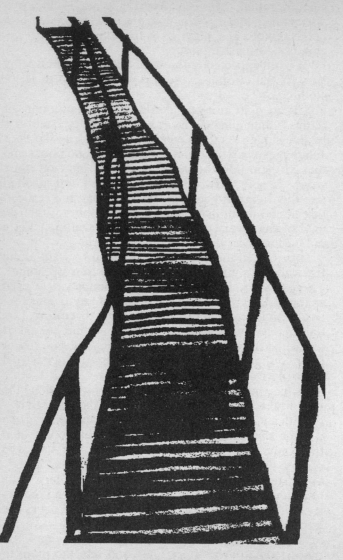

Vine Ladder

the front of the room. Once Julian was seated, Buold announced that the meal should begin. The others found their way to tables and when they were seated, the serving of the meal began.

Each table returned to conversation giving occasional glances to Julian at the elders table. Julian felt slightly uncomfortable.

"So you are of the South. Which place?" an older Dweller next to Buold leaned over and was asking.

"Jard. In the Middle World."

"That is a long distance from here! You must be exhausted." All within earshot were fascinated, having never journeyed beyond the Forest.

"A little, but I'm fine now. Have you ever been to Jard?"

The table conversation went on, all of it cordial and very similar. Julian could tell by the politeness that this was a very special occasion. It wasn't often that the Dwellers would welcome Southlanders, especially ones that were rumored to be of the Ones of the Palace and hold great magic. Not one word of any conversation held with him during the meal, or the entertainment that followed however, hinted at such things. The Dwellers were very formal as a tribe. Any inquiry into such a personal area would be considered rude and offensive!

The evening meal was long. Buold, noticing that Julian was getting drowsy, motioned to Quei to escort their guest home. He unobtrusively leaned over and bade him good eve and told him he would see him off in the early sun rise. Julian left after parting pleasantries, to retire. There were more hardships to come in the next sun.

It was not very long after Julian had gone, that a message arrived, scribbled on a piece of yellow leaf paper. Buold took it, and under the eyes of the other Elders read silently:

Fon, reports three more like the first. Much stronger in the ways of the others. They will be sent on in the sun rise.

"Is something wrong Buold?" one elder casually asked, amidst the revelry of the meal.

"It has begun. There are more in the Forest headed this way," a serious mood fell upon them.

"How long before we are known here to all who enter the Forest. So far these are friends, but what if the others, who the traveler spoke of, are also in the Forest? What can we do?"

"Tell your sentries at every point within the Forest to send message of any who enter, no matter who, or for how long they remain in the forest. The least we can do is be forewarned of their presence. As long as the numbers remain small, we will cope. Whoever enters, if not a friend, will never be permitted to tell of their entry," the others understood, "We must revive the horrors of the Burning Forest to the outer Worlds, if we are to survive!"

"And of the Darker magic he mentioned?" asked the same.

"And the red books that Quei saw him put into his pocket?" then another.

"Let us hope that this Julian completes his journey before the need for concern in that area is desperately upon us. There is much to be explained here, even I have noticed a changing within. The dream is strong. In the sun rising I will hurry him on. We must try to slow any who follow, in case they are not what they seem and trick us into helping both sides, whoever they are."

All the Dwellers could do now, was wait and hope for the rapid completion of Julian's purpose. In the early part of the sun rising Buold would bid Julian farewell, but he would take the precaution of not telling him of the others that were to arrive by that mid sun. Buold wanted a chance to evaluate first hand the authenticity of these three. If they were friends, he would send them along after Julian, if they weren't...

- - - - - - - - - - - - - - - - - - -

Suddenly there came a prodding in his side, and a loud shouting voice.

"Get up you filthy Gott!" It was early morning, and Merm had been discovered by the newly arrived sentries to the Forest.

"Get away, you..." Merm, still half asleep, believed he was in Norkleau. A couple of more stern prods and he angrily awoke, stopping short from screaming at whoever had dared to disturb him, when he saw and realized the situation.

"Get up you filthy Gott!" repeated the order.

Merm complied. He could make out weapons and three creatures of the wood. These were the Dwellers in their camouflage, but Merm was unacquainted with them.

"Who are you, and why are you here?!" It was not really a question.

Merm decided to play his identity down, "I am a farmer of the Gottland. I entered the Forest to find my Doca and became lost. (A Doca was a pet. It had fur, a long tail and was the size of an average Jard. Its teeth were menacing and it smelt. A good pet for a Gott!). Have you seen him?"

"You will come with us." It was as if the Dweller had not heard a word.

Merm did not speak, but did what he was told. He fell in between them and they marched into the Forest. How fortunate that they had found him. Soon he would be with the thief. He planned to walk along with them until they had returned to their Forest home, then he would use the magic of the box to escape from their sight. No one would be able to stop him from sightlessly following and finding the Key. Once it was around his neck, he would no longer require the shield of invisibility. Everything was going according to his dreams!

- - - - - - - - - - - - - - - - -

In the southern tip of the Forest, amongst the

Moonfruit Pine, Darla was the first to awake. She was totally rested. While she waited for Thiunn and Eruinn to awaken, she had a quick walk around the raised ground. The old Moonfruit Fon, was the largest Pine. All the other wood in the vicinity was younger, smaller Pine.

"What is it that you search for?" Fon was communing. He rather enjoyed being able to commune with this traveler. It was so direct and easy.

"Just having a look around. Tell me, you seem to be the only wood of age. Why is that?"

"Long ago there were many of my kind. We were open and accepting of all. They were cut by the ones from the South for profit. Many perished. It was the Ones from the Palace that saved the few that remain. They helped to re-seed, but it will take a very long time in the measurement of your kind till these young Pine are fully grown. I was one of the few scattered surviving Pine. It has been my task to care and rear these Pine to maturity."

"I see. I wish you well in your duty, but if we do not find the other that came by and help him to complete his task, then all of this will not matter anymore." Darla walked back to Thiunn and Eruinn who were still asleep.

"You must travel through that field and then straight north through the Forest. You will soon be met by the Dwellers. They will take you to the Stoneman."

"Thank you Fon. I hope we will meet again. I would like to hear more of those times in this Pine."

"Upon your return we will speak of these." Fon stopped its communing.

Darla was standing over the two Chosen Ones, "Get up you two. It is getting late. We would like to get where we are going by the mid sun.

"Is it that time again?" Eruinn complained, "This is the best sleep I have had in ages."

"Me too," Thiunn was now awake.

The Moonfruit had given the three a deep, protected,

rejuvenating rest. It had sensed their need and also began not to question their presence. Old memories were flowing through its sap. These, like the Stoneman who had earlier passed, carried the honor of the others. They were to be quietly helped in any way possible. This had been communicated to the Dwellers, who would meet these three and protect them as they had Julian. These three were of no threat, and carried the power of the Old Ones. Fon knew this and as they left it, watched, wondering if the Forests would ever recapture the glory of those Old Ones that lived deep within them. Soon, Darla and the nephews were out of the reach of Fon's sense.

It did not take long for the newly posted sentries, who had also been alerted by Fon the previous eve, to meet them. Eruinn was in the lead and Darla the rear. They had been chopping their way through the undergrowth of the Forest. Eruinn and Thiunn, who had never seen such trees, were humbled by their majesty. Some trunks were as wide as ten Jardians! They felt as insignificant as the tiniest creatures in comparison. The weight of the age of the collective trees was awesome!

During their trek, while their eyes were more above than on the surface, the sentries had spied them. They circled round them. After an appropriate time of observation and confirmation that these were the three of the 'sensing' from the Moonfruit, and of no danger, the Dwellers jumped out from behind two medium sized trunks.

"Hello. You must be the guests that we have expected." A cheery svelte Dweller stood before them. The surprise of his apparition almost made Eruinn and Thiunn fall back. At the next instant another popped out from behind another smaller trunk with similar greeting. They weren't sure of what to expect next!

"Do not be afraid. We are Dwellers in this Forest and are here to guide you to our home and your friend.

I am called Gitec, and that is Fevol." Fevol politely touched two fingers to his temple as a salutation. These were the 'guests' that like Julian, would be taken to the village without being blindfolded.

"I am Darla, and this is Eruinn," who was still breath taken, "and this Thiunn."

Thiunn timidly said hello, "Are we very far from our friend?"

"No, if you are up to a slightly faster pace, we will reach there by mid sun." Gitec had a magnetic personality. Just these few words had been uttered and now they all felt as if they were friends of long standing.

"That will be fine. The sooner we arrive the better."

"Fevol, take up the rear," then to the three, "Follow me. If you need to rest, just call out." Before anyone could acknowledge he had leapt off!

- - - - - - - - - - - - - - - - - -

The Forest was magnificent! Julian was spellbound by its size and grandeur. The north end was full of the oldest trunks, which rose so high that it was hard to make out the sky. Below was just trunk after trunk. The ground was dry and barren of green. Not enough light ever reached this level to support vegetation. The surface was soft with the settled and untouched dead leaves from the lofty branches. Occasionally there was a rotten stump. As they walked, there was the absorbed spongy sound of peat. The air was still and full of the mossy smell of the wood and peat. There was not a sound other than their steps. Julian found it invigorating.

Eventually, off in the distance came a soothing sound. It was difficult to identify and it grew louder and louder, till finally Julian placed it as running water. Fast running water. *There must be an incredible river ahead.* The sound grew louder and still there was no end to the Forest. They kept moving forward.

The sound became so loud it was impossible to hear anything else. A cool caressing chill ran down Julian's back and shoulders. The sense of great power and danger was conveyed by that loud a rush of water. They moved on.

As well as the sound of the river, came the strong smell of water. It could not be far now. Julian just managed to make out the hint of a very dark line. The line became larger till they had come to the end of this side of the Forest and the banks of the Pass River.

It was ominous! There was at least a hundred lengths to its other bank and another solid wall of Forest. The water was strong and dark. It undulated with great speed. Julian stepped back from the edge of it lest he lose his footing and tumble in. He was not a swimmer, but even a strong swimmer would not survive in that cruel water! As far as his eye could see there was Forest on either side and the river. He wondered what Quei and Thodox would do and how they were to cross it?

"Quite a sight!" Quei was yelling over the sound of the wet rush and pointing to the dark midnight blue water.

Julian nodded, "I've never seen anything as scary! You don't expect me to cross this do you?! I don't think we can cross this here!"

"We will walk up there," Thod pointed along the bank, "careful not to slip. The ground isn't very solid. There is a bend and the river narrows farther along. It will be a place to cross."

Julian shook his head indicating he understood, "Don't worry. I don't plan on slipping into that!"

"Good. Let's move on. Stay close together and keep your concentration on the bank. Don't let the river distract you. It is a narrow path that we must take. It is the only way!" Quei went first, carefully making his way. Julian and Thodox came behind.

It was scary! The power of the river drew one and at the same time repelled. Julian felt tempted to fall in just to sense the oneness of the rolling strength! He knew this was just the natural attraction that such an absorbing power of any kind would have. He resisted the call.

The bank ran straight along the river; the Forest, tight to the edge. There was barely enough room to pass and in some places they were forced to walk across tree trunks that had fallen from the weakness of the soft wet soil unable to support their towering weight. Other trees were no longer alive, having been forced to exist in such wetness, and others still, had been swept from their rooting during the times of the river's rising. This was all easily seen by the water marks on the sides.

Quei and Thodox were not used to such a place. They also found the path precarious! Their clothing was accumulating dirt from the slips and lost footings of the excursion. *When would this end!* Quei halted to look ahead, allowing the others to catch up. They stood on a rise about two lengths from the water. They were out of breath and the effort of shouting after the roughness of the hike made them very utilitarian in their communication.

"Okay?" Quei held up his left hand with thumb up. He was checking his companions, especially Julian. They both responded using the same sign language. "Not far," Quei using his other hand pointed from the part of the river that they had just traversed along and up ahead. He was implying that there was to be some change coming. Again Thodox and Julian signed *'Okay'*.

"We stop again there! Before we cross." Again the communication was verbal, accompanied with sign. Quei made semi-elliptical motions with his right hand and forefinger to show crossing over from one side to the other. Thodox and Julian nodded their understanding, which also indicated the end to the chat. Quei turned and motioned them on.

- - - - - - - - - - - - - - - - - -

Dorluc had by chance been watching the view screen as it had once more located Julian with the two Dwellers in the north end of the Burning Forest. He watched as they passed through the Forest. When they arrived at the Pass River, he understood what was transpiring before his eyes. The thief was headed for Tika! This must be stopped! There weren't any of his allies close enough to be of assistance. Dorluc was in a panic. If they managed to cross the river and eventually enter the zone of Tika, it would be impossible for him to influence the outcome. Merm would be left, without much magic or power, to his own resources against the Magic of the Chosen Ones. He paced in front of the screen. He would have to risk identifying himself close to the zone and use his influence to prevent the crossing. He turned back to the view screen and waited for his opportunity.

- - - - - - - - - - - - - -

Just as Quei had indicated, the bank started to follow the river as it bent more directly north. From their vantage, it was also obvious that there was a narrow point in the river ahead and the water ran slower. There were dark black boulders the size of houses sitting comfortably amidst the stream of water. Though the gaps between were large, it would be possible to make a crossing! Seeing the end to the walk the three quickened their pace. Soon they had covered the distance and were standing together on the bank looking over the water to the first boulder. The noise of the river was greatly reduced and a sense of calm pervaded.

"It seemed alot easier from back there." Thodox was disappointed.

"We might have to get a bit wet to get to the first rock, but after that we should be able to stay out of the water for the others." Quei was planning ahead. This is what made him such a sought after companion when

The River Crossing

in the Forest. Any Dweller felt safe in his capable experienced care.

"But I don't swim," Julian calmly said. He silently

decided that there would have to be another way. As far as the Dwellers were concerned, he would soon learn to swim!

- - - - - - - - - - - - - - - -

Dorluc was still watching. This was an opportunity. As he waited, Dorluc was not alert to the fact that this thief might sense his presence, he merely sought a chance to stop the crossing, and would therefore be unprepared for any other eventuality. In his view screen room he closed his eyes and concentrated on the image of the river.

- - - - - - - - - - - - - - - -

Quei, as usual, was first to wade into the river, which dropped off in a stride or two so that he was unable to touch the stony bed. Moving his arms to keep himself above water with all the weight of his pack and wet heavy clothing, he slowly found his way to the first boulder. Grabbing hold of its slimy surface he pulled his weight out of the river and flat onto the slope of the slab. Julian was to go next, but from the fear of the depths of the dark water, hesitated. In doing so valuable time was being given to Dorluc. Under the Evil's influence the river was becoming choppy and rough. It was beginning to resemble a lake in stormy conditions.

Julian was confused. If he waited much longer the swim would be more tricky! He felt a push and splash he was in the water. But Thodox had not shoved him in! It was Dorluc! Julian struggled to keep himself afloat and instead of passing to the awaiting grip of Quei, was being pulled by the water down and along the river to it's fuller strength! Quei and Thodox called out, but he did not hear amidst his struggle and his bobbing in the water. Julian was now drifting and picking up speed toward the middle of the river!

Thodox signaled Quei to get to the other bank, while he went down the other side. They had to hurry before the river was too wide and fast to do anything. Neither had a thought of what they could do, but they wanted to keep visual contact. Perhaps something would turn up.

Julian was now entering the rougher water. Thodox and Quei were trying to make him understand to try slowly to work with the current and drift to one of the banks. Once there, either could grab hold of him and pull him out. Julian understood, but every time he tried, some greater force pulled him back to the center. He kept bobbing and gasping for air! He didn't recognize that Dorluc was the force!

Thodox and Quei were still running along the bank to keep pace with Julian. He would not last if he couldn't get to a bank soon. Every time his head went below the surface, it was longer till he popped back up. 'He can't die!' Each of the Dwellers independently thought. They kept watching and running. Julian was being swept far away! Under he went again, and again and again...this last time he failed to surface.

The two Dwellers on the banks were horrified by the prospects of losing Julian. The more they ran after and along, the harder it seemed to catch up. Julian was going down deeper. It was not right! The change in the river had been too sudden and Julian's efforts should have been bringing at least some tiny result! They had to find a way to save him! A tremendous panic was taking hold. This shouldn't be happening!

- - - - - - - - - - - - - - - - - -

Dorluc was using his influence to drag and keep the thief under. Once he was drowned, Merm could be shown the place to find this troublesome body and take back what was taken. Julian struggled and tried not to waste any of the last breath he had taken before being pulled under.

When he had gone under and was held in place, preventing him from rising to the surface, a voice spoke clearly to him.

"Do not be afraid. It is the Evil that holds you. Take hold of the Key."

Julian fumbled to find the Key that he had tied into his pocket. Taking hold of it meant giving up one hand that might pull him to the surface. He trusted the voice and did what it had directed.

- - - - - - - - - - - - - - - - - -

Quei and Thodox searched both sides of the river for any sign of Julian. They were still in shock. Neither he nor Quei spoke. Never had this happened to them! Never had they lost a companion in their care. The search along the bank had been exhaustive. Every aspect of its winding examined; every fallen trunk or half submerged branch pulled aside. They had spent most of the time after the mid sun searching. Finally, accepting the inevitable, and exhausted by the events, they were forced to make camp for the night. They could search no longer. Julian was not found! He was probably far away and enroute to the Marshlands by now!

Thodox collected dry vines and wood and started a small fire to warm some drink and heat food. They both sat silently, Not a word was uttered between them. When it had become dark, they said their goodnights and rolled over to try to sleep—they could not! Quietly they thought of their companion, dreading that terrible way to die! In the morning they would return to the tribe and explain.

- - - - - - - - - - - - - - - - - -

Dorluc was exuberant as he watched from his realm! By using the Magic he had prevented the thief from any further interference. It would now be easy to locate the body and the Key using the screen and directing Merm. With the deed done, Dorluc decided to leave the view screen room for a rest. As he closed the door behind him he laughed an evil chortle. He once again felt superior to those mere Jardians! As he left in his arrogance he remembered that he forgot to turn off the view screen. He would leave it on for a short time unattended. He was in control again, now that the threat of the thief was gone. He exited the room not noticing that the view screen which had been filled with the display of the limp body of Julian submerged beneath the River, suddenly change, and the limp figure disappear as if by Magic! The threat was not gone!

- - - - - - - - - - - - - - - - - -

Julian had found the Key which was still where he had hidden it in his pocket. In using his arms to search, the force under the river completely overtook his body. He was being sucked deeper into its depths! He had taken hold of the Key in hope of some Magical rescue. None ensued. His breath was lean, and his mind was screaming out for fresh oxygen. Just when he thought he would explode, a voice was again present.

"Do not be afraid. Allow the moment to pass. You will not perish." Julian had no other option but do as the voice beckoned. He relaxed and allowed his being to go limp. *"Think of the surface. Think of the bank."* He complied with the voice. He imagined that he was sitting on the bank on the other side of the narrows where the boulders were to allow the crossing. More and more he saw himself there. It was strange. The more he visualized himself actually there, the more comfortable he was in the water. His concern for fresh air was diminishing. This encouraged him to concentrate more till the only reality in his mind was of him-

self on the other side of the river sitting on shore. It became more and more real. He closed his eyes. More and more he imagined the scene. Soon he did not even hear the muffled sound of the water all around him, or even its feel. He concentrated further. He actually began to hear the cool night breeze and feel the air blowing against his wet body. He thought to open his eyes, but was afraid to break the vision, his only hope of relief!

He kept this up for what seemed an eternity. Finally, he could not withstand the temptation to see where he had been pulled by the river. He opened his eyes—he was sitting on the bank on the other side of the river! He patted himself to check if it was a dream. It was real! Somehow the magic within the Key had saved him! He then panicked realizing that the *Evil* had found him. He considered, in his dazed state, whether or not he should turn invisible, not realizing that the *Evil* had ended its watch! He then reasoned if the *Evil* had found him and had not been successful in its attempt to drown him, then there must be a greater power helping him now. He felt compelled to trust in that power. Something inside was reassuring him. Julian had no way of understanding how the Key along with his thoughts had worked this miracle. He wasn't sure he could duplicate it, and he hoped he would not need to. It was a horrifying experience down in that wet darkness! His attention returned to his wet person. With the night breeze, he was starting to shiver. He hadn't survived the crossing to die from exposure!

He patted himself down once more and noticed the books. They were still safe. He paused and took in a new sampling of the breathing world. There was a different smell in the air. Smoke? Yes that was it. A fire was alight nearby. Standing up he scanned the area for any sight of light. Seeing none, he tried to follow the smell of the burning vines. He noisily made his way. At about a hundred lengths, there was a fire. Immediately his mind fell on Quei and Thodox. Picking up his pace he ran to the fire, but when he arrived no one was there. Disappointed by the vacant camp, he sat by the fire. The chill was too much to take. He was beginning to warm up when:

"That fire is ours! I wouldn't get too comfortable!" came a familiar voice from behind him.

Jumping up and turning, Julian faced the campers. Upon realizing that they were all standing together again on the other side of the bank, and were not some transients passing by, they spoke out enthusiastically all at once: "Quei, Julian, Thodox!"

- - - - - - - - - - - - - - - - - - -

The sentries from the eastern boarder were pleased to have found such a foul creature as this Gott. They were almost back and ready to report, when he disappeared right before their very eyes! Spellbound by the mystery they backtracked and searched the area. He was nowhere to be found. As they were so close to home and it was getting quite dark, they decided to continue on and make a report.

Merm went along just back twenty lengths from them. How easy it had been to trick these fools! They were leading him right to their secret place deep within the Forest. He would remember the way, and after he controlled the magic of the Key, return to teach some Gott manners to these vile creatures who had treated the Lord of the Gotts with such disregard!

Chapter 8.

A chill ran through Darla as the three entered the secret Forest home of the Dwellers. It was enervating. It had taken the whole morning to travel the distance from the Moonfruit to the forest home of the Dwellers. High above, the sun was just past it's mid point and their escorts, who were friendly but not extremely communicative, were taking them to Buold. Buold wanted to verify their connection with Julian. But this wasn't the reason for Darla's apprehension. There was a hint of the *Evil*, she didn't know exactly its source, but it didn't belong here! They were taken to a ground level home amongst the thick tree trunks. There they were told to wait, rest and refresh themselves with food that would be brought.

They were to be taken to the Head Elder as soon as he was available. It was a long wait. Finally, by the beginning of the eve, Gitcc and Fevol knocked at the door of their confinement and announced that they were to follow them. Darla was displeased with the wait, which in her mind had been intentional and unnecessary. They could not afford to waste time!

Buold greeted them in the same tree top home that Julian had been taken, upon his earlier arrival. The sight was just as awesome to these next 'guests', as it had been for Julian.

"I am Buold. Welcome to our home."

"Darla, and this is Eruinn and Thiunn. We have come in search of another." Darla was describing Julian when Buold interrupted.

"How can we help?"

"We need to find him, he is in grave danger and will require our presence. There are others who follow after us all. He is only one, we are three."

"Three?..."

While they spoke, outside and below them the two sentries who had captured Merm were returning. There was a commotion as they were greeted and began to speak of the strangeness of their loss. They were not aware that Merm was right there following, invisible to all, trying with great effort to contain himself.

"How stupid these creatures are!" he whispered to himself as he watched the antics.

After a few more moments of conversation, the sentries began moving toward Buold's tree top lift. Once there, they pushed the hidden communication button and waited.

"Yes," came a deep raspy voice of one of Buold's aides.

"Sentry post East to report to Buold, sir."

"I'm sending down. Please come up." Buold's aide had been told to admit any of the sentries to report the moment they arrived, no matter what the interruption. The aide sent the lift down, then turned away from the intercom to inform Buold. He walked into the larger room where the three of the Southworlders were being interviewed.

"Excuse me, sir," the interruption broke off Buold's response to the 'three', "Sentries to report. They are on the way up."

"Thank you. Send them right in." Buold resumed his sentence with Darla, "How is it that you come to us? How do I know you are not the danger that you speak of?"

"We ask in the name of Three." Out of nowhere Eruinn spoke, but it was not the same everyday voice his companions were used to. It was more powerful and loud. "We are of the Ones of the Palace and speak through this one to ask the Dwellers for passage."

Everyone was taken aback. So many strange things had been happening lately to all of them. Darla was quick to understand what was going on and added, "We are all together and must protect great magic. Can you lead us to the Stoneman?"

Buold was in thought, still not sure of everything, when the noise of the lift doors opening reached through to him. He saw and beckoned the light, sure footed sentries from the lift into his presence. This additional interruption forced the conversation to hang with Eruinn's uttering of the word 'three'...

"Sir, we report the loss of a Gott."

"A Gott? Lost? Explain."

"We discovered a big Gott in the eastern Forest along the border of the Gotts. He claimed to be a lost farmer. We decided to bring him here, as those were the standing orders for any new entrants to the Forest. Everything was fine. Then just as we came into the area, he escaped."

"What do you mean escaped? Why didn't you go after him?"

"Well... he disappeared."

"How could anything as smelly and large as a Gott just disappear?"

"He vanished. Right before our eyes. One moment he was walking between us and the next he was gone!"

This caught the attention of Darla and the two nephews. Darla asked, "Can you describe this Gott?"

The sentry gave a look to Buold as if he was questioning who this female was to be so bold. Buold nodded to indicate that the sentry should answer.

"Yes. A much larger Gott than we have ever seen. Smelly, but better kempt than most. He spoke like one of command, not a farmer. His eyes were dark, and he wore a dark cape. Boots..."

"Boots? Anything on the boots?" Darla pushed.

"Yes a strange insignia in red, matching a ring on

his right forefinger."

"It is him." Darla spoke to Eruinn and Thiunn, "It is the one from Norkleau. When he was pulling at me I noticed the very same ring."

"Who is this one?" Buold stopped the sentry by a wave of his hand, from speaking further. He directed his words to Darla, Eruinn ,and Thiunn. "Who is this Gott?"

"It is the Lord of the Gotts himself!" Thiunn answered.

"The Lord of the Gotts here? Why?" Buold said unbelieving.

"He wants to find Julian. Julian carries secrets of the Old and he wants them. He must be found and prevented from acquiring that knowledge," Thiunn's tone was worried.

"You must help us to find Julian! The danger is closer than we expected. If the Gott Lord knows of this place there will soon be much trouble here. We must find Julian before it is too late!" Darla, feeling that Buold was now convinced of the truth of their story, demanded his help.

"We can lead you in the same direction as he went. He left early in the sun rise and is not far. There will be..."

A cup which had been on the table suddenly fell over unto the floor and broke. The unusualness of the action prompted silence and attention from them all. Darla looked to Buold. "We are not alone!"

And they weren't. Merm who had been following the sentries to the lift, had decided to climb on top of it and ride to the tree top and find out what he could. It had been so easy. The sentries had noticed a strong aroma, but wrote it off to their own perspiration from the long trip back. They hadn't had a chance to wash or change. After reaching the top Merm had carefully followed them into the room. —They were here! The thieves! He remembered the female well from

Norkleau. She had taken the Key and passed it onto the other two Southlanders!

It had not been hard to listen, but the room was too small and he was clumsy. The cup was knocked over as he tried to keep out of the way of the unsuspecting others in the room. He stood motionless in anticipation of discovery, but it was his stench that gave him away.

"What's that smell?" Darla asked of all.

"We have not yet had a chance to refresh..." the sentry who had done all the talking began to apologize and was cut short.

"No, not you. Something else! Stronger, dirtier!"

They all strained their noises to detect the distinctive smell. Each walking in the direction that the odor identified to their senses. Merm remained still, clutching the box which gave him the invisibility. He would have to make a dash for the lift to elude them.

"That smell! Can you find It? Its the smell of a Gott!"

Upon Darla's identification Merm panicked. All of them were honing in upon his spot. If they physically found him, he would never be able to find or reclaim the Key! He decided to make a rush for the lift the first opening he got.

All of the others in the room weren't sure what to believe, but there was definitely a strange smell which was not of any present. They began to close in on the invisible Merm without knowing what to expect. Then, just as Darla was about to collide into him, Merm made a dash pushing aside any in his pathway. There was complaining, on the part of the pushed aside Dwellers to each other, wondering who had been shoving.

"Over there!" Eruinn called out as he sensed the passage of something headed for the lift. The lift door opened and closed.

The party ran after, in an attempt to stop the lift from

completion of its travel, but to no avail. Whoever or whatever it was, was gone! They all stood as they watched the lift arrive below. The door opened and closed, but no one exited.

"Someone was here," Darla informed, "Somehow the Gott Lord has obtained some powerful magic. We must be careful not to lead him to finding Julian. He is still among us here in your home. We may not be able to see him, but we can smell him. We will have to take special precautions to try to stop him from following."

"We can use the wild forest Dologs. They have far superior ability than us in tracking scents. They will keep a nose out for this invisible Gott. If they detect him, even his invisibility will not stop their teeth from finding a hide to sink in to. This Gott Lord will not be able to be anywhere close to us." Buold smiled at the thought of unleashing these vicious reptiles upon a Gott.

"Good. Can you now help us find Julian?" Darla would not wait any longer. They must continue into the night to find Julian.

Upon reaching the forest floor, Merm had scampered away as fast as he could run. He kept running till he felt confident that nobody was in pursuit. He stopped to rest, and as he did so he let go of his grip on the box and instantly became visible. It did not matter, there were no eyes hereabouts. If someone did come, he would merely use the magic of the box again!

There was now a dilemma. The thieves were wise to his presence. That meant that he would now have more difficulty in tracking them. Certainly, precautions would be taken and he would now have to be extremely watchful not to be caught. Somehow he must find his way back and continue to follow wherever the thieves went. He had not come this far to lose them!

He lay back and gazed into the tree tops. How remarkable a hideaway this place was. Never would he have considered such a hiding place for a city. When this was all through, he would return to this place and destroy these Dwellers! First, he must finish *this* task. He had to find a way to disguise his smell. They might use Dologs. He surveyed the peat moss in the area where he rested and noticed a Liptuys tree. The Liptuys tree was very pungent, and combined with the peat would do the job. He gathered some large leaves and peat and began to crush and mix them together. The moisture from the juice of the Liptuys gradually turned the mix into a crude lumpy lotion. Merm began applying it all over himself. When he had finished and was satisfied that he was covered, he began his return to the Dwellers' home. He would be careful and follow the thieves until the Key was revealed and he had an opportunity to reclaim it.

- - - - - - - - - - - - - - - - - -

The realization that the *Evil* of the Gotts was once again on their trail disturbed the Southlanders. Darla now understood the chill she had earlier felt. It had been a warning. Darla felt foolish that she had neglected to pay closer attention to this sensing. From now on they must all begin to trust their new sensing and inner voices.

"He will be back soon. The Gotts are very crafty and know many tricks. We must find Julian!" Darla was partially involved with her own inner abilities of trying to determine any other threats. There were none.

"Your friend has traveled north and is headed for Tika. Two of the best Dweller guides are escorting him to the entrance to the paths. From there he will be on his own. We can also lead you there, but no other than the Ones of the Palace may pass along that route." Buold was prophetic.

"How long will it take to get there?"

"One sun rise."

"Then Julian is half a sun rise ahead. Can we go now?"

"Yes. Gitec and Fevol can show the way." Buold turned to Gitec, "Show them the way, and return with Quei and Thodox."

"Yes sir."

Turning back to Darla and the nephews, "I will have provisions prepared. May the strength of the Three be with you in your quest and make you successful."

Darla, Eruinn and Thiunn spent a few moments thanking Buold and when an aide re-entered with provisions, they, along with Gitec and Fevol, went to the lift, opened its door and descended to the Forest floor. New hope was alive in them. They felt that they were close to Julian and that they would still be able to prevent the *Evil* from acquiring the Key or the *Passwords*. The worlds would be safe again soon! As they disappeared into the Forest, Buold couldn't help but think he would never see any of them again!

- - - - - - - - - - - - - - - - - -

Rmont was tired. There had been no stop since the rest, before entering the Burning Forest. It had been a long ride. Not one of the party of Riders had uttered a sound; their full attention had been upon the Forest and any creatures that may have been lurking within. Gorg had ridden in front with Rmont. Any noise that issued forth caused the whole party of seven to slow their pace and strain their observational talents. Nothing had happened. Nothing had stirred. They all felt relieved when finally at the end of the sun rise they exited the Forest and found themselves in the Bad Land.

The Bad Land was a rocky barren maze. It stretched to the beginnings of the mountain canyons providing an excellent barrier to the uninvited. The seven would have to continue through it impeded by its unwelcoming treacherous paths. Rmont was tired.

"We should stop here. I don't think it wise to cross these lands in the dark." Rmont was not asking Gorg.

"Easy is. Hurry must. Falls of Light close are." Gorg had been through land like this before and didn't want to stop the momentum that the Riders had settled into. The Falls of Light were northwest from here and they could be reached by the middle of the night. He preferred to get there and then stop. This spot was still too near to the Burning Forest and he and his Six would be happier away from here. Traversing the Bad Land was far more pleasant a thought, than remaining and setting up a camp for the eve. There wasn't a Rider who didn't prefer to continue on, in spite of his fatigue!

"It will be dangerous to go on when we are tired."

"If stay more dangerous is. Forest close is. We will go!"

That being said, the discussion was over. Gorg rode ahead accompanied by his Six. Rmont reluctantly fell into the rear. They would be at the falls that night.

- - - - - - - - - - - - - - - - - -

"What happened to you!? We thought you were dead!" Quei was thrilled.

"After the last time you went under, we ran along the banks, but you never surfaced! It's good to have you back!" Thodox was showing his fondness for this brave little Southworlder.

"I must have become tangled in the undertow." Julian would not mention the voices, "Next, I was holding my breath and being pulled deeper and farther along. I thought it was the end. Just when my breath was going, the undertow weakened and I pulled myself to the surface and eventually drifted to the bank. I was going to make my way across the rocks and head back in search of you when I noticed the smell of your fire. I wasn't sure if it was you two, and that's why I crept up!"

"All that matters is that you are well and here, and finally on this side!" Quei laughed. "Couldn't you have crossed like us! For someone who hates water you sure got wet! You gave us a heck of a fright!"

They were all laughing now at the humor of the crossing. Julian was the only one who knew the truth and the nearness of the *Evil*. He would keep it a secret for now. They continued talking, and Thodox began to brew a pot of warm drink.

- - - - - - - - - - - - - - - - - -

The Forest was dark. Darla, Eruinn, and Thiunn stayed close to Gitec and Fevol. There hadn't been a sound all the time since they left Buold and the Dwellers' home. They were stretching their limits, but Gitec had said they were very close to the Pass River. That was where Quei and Thodox had taken Julian. They moved on at a fast pace.

Gradually a low constant rumble was audible.

"What's that noise?" Thiunn asked.

"We are almost at the Pass River." Gitec was out of breath as he answered.

"We will stop there to rest, once we have come to the bridge of rocks," Fevol continued.

"How far ahead will the others be by now?" Eruinn questioned.

"That is hard to say. Probably they are half way to the Falls of Light. Don't worry we will catch up. We will not camp this night, just rest then move on," Gitec tried to comfort the young Southlander.

"Yes. The others would camp, so we have an advantage to catch up if we don't stop long," Fevol also tried to help.

They kept walking. The sound of the river grew louder and louder. It was soothing and sent shivers up the back. The three felt warm and drowsy. The sound became so loud that they had to shout if they wanted to communicate. Their awe of this majestic wonder of nature, was very much like Julian's earlier encountering!

Gitec and Fevol motioned to the three to come up to where they had just stopped. It was very dark, but as they approached, a sparkling light could be seen. The Pass River! The light from the night stars reflected in the river's snake like twisting motion. What a sight to behold! They stood not speaking, absorbing the scene as best they could in the darkness.

The Pass River was old. The legends spoke of it as a river of magic. The magic of the people of Tika. It was said to flow from the center of Tika along the canyon valleys, through the Marshland and then underground to eventually feed the Lake of Choices. It was ominous in its underlying power.

The name Pass referred to the separation of the Good from the *Evil*. From the accepted to the outcast. In the Forest and the other lower lands it was just a powerful force of water, but in the northern portion it carved its way through deep chasms. The only place to cross and thereby gain access to the paths to Tika, was at the Falls of Light. Only good intention could pass unchallenged.

Tika was a preserve of the knowledge and wisdom of the Old Ones. The Balance was maintained there and any threat to it not welcome. Passing through the Falls of Light, those who entered could be screened. To those undesirable who were prohibited entry, only the treacherous paths would open. The treacherous paths led to dead ends and insurmountable climbs. This would force those of questionable of intention to return and not attempt to continue the journey to Tika. To the welcomed, opened the tunnels which safely led to the center of the city. The Pass River was the dividing line, a boundary, a test after which only the good were granted passage.

"We will go up," Gitec was shouting and trying to motion the direction of their route, "to the rocks where we can cross. Be careful. The bank is narrow and in places falls away."

The three didn't need cautioning. Though the river was caressing, none wished any closer physical contact. They nodded acknowledgment. One by one they progressed along the bank.

- - - - - - - - - - - - - - - - - -

Julian was still drinking from his warm mug listening to Thodox as he told old stories.

"I was alone and about to make camp for the night. The eve was much like this, when a loud grunting sound came from behind. I turned and there was the biggest Stilat you have ever seen, its teeth all bared deciding to make me it's meal," Both Quei and Julian were enjoying the fireside tales, "I jumped around, grabbed a piece of burning wood from the fire and tossed it into the furry beast. The Stilat gave out a yelp, turned and ran, rubbing against anything it could to extinguish the smoking fur!"

"Now, that is not what I call a story!" Quei was jovial.

"You think you can do better?" Thod was challenging, Quei expected it. This was their way. Julian sat amused.

"Fine. Here goes!

"Deep in the Forest in the most untouched parts I was chasing a Reebol," he described for Julian's benefit, "a tiny little ferreting creature. Makes good stew. Just as I was about to catch hold of the slow thing, I came face to face with a large forest Ursa, with five of its young. Well, we were both startled! Feeling endangered, she rose up and took her attack stance. I was mortified. There was no out running an angry Ursa, and climbing a tree was crazy since she was better suited to climb. I decided to drop right there on the spot and stay motionless. In doing so the Ursa dropped her stance and, bewildered, approached to investigate. I'll never forget the sniff and snort she did. I felt like screaming out. Then without a sound she turned and returned to her now wandering young. After a short time, when she had clearly left, I rose up and continued my chase of the Reebol!"

"You sure can weave a tale!" Thod was shaking his head and smiling, "I've never heard such lies in my life!"

"And you call what you said the truth!?" All of them were enjoying the late night. It was like being young again without a care or worry.

"What about you, Julian? Any stories you care to tell?" Quel was inquisitive.

"Well, I'm not as good as you two, but I'll give it a shot!

"Let me see…It was long ago, in a time when not many traveled in the South. My father and I went on an excursion to visit close friends. We made camp the first night in the bush near the path…"

- - - - - - - - - - - - - - - - -

They made it to the boulders quickly. The water was calmer, and the noise of the river subdued.

"This is the place. It would be wise to cross in the sun rise. We should make camp here." Gitec was right of course. To attempt a crossing in the dark with the Southlanders, would be inviting disaster.

"How about there," Darla pointed out a circular area near the bank that was sheltered by four large trunks.

"Yes that will do. Eruinn and Thiunn can gather some kindling for the fire. Okay?" Gitec peered over to the two, "Don't wander too far."

"Sure. Let's go Eruinn." Thiunn welcomed the chance to be finally appreciated and not ignored as youngsters, as had been the case so far. The Dwellers did not pay them much heed or solicit opinion from them. Even Buold had politely ignored and omitted them!

Eruinn followed Thiunn, as they went to their task. They went up the bank, around the curve, and searched for burning material.

"What was that?" Eruinn noticed a faint noise.

"What was what?" Thiunn wasn't interested in the imagination of his younger brother.

"That sound, it's coming from across there. Sounds like laughter."

"Laughter. Get real. There isn't anyone other than us here!"

"Maybe not, but how do you explain that?" Eruinn now pointed out the small flicker of a flame. Thiunn strained and they understood. "Yes. It might be Uncle Julian! What do you think?" Thiunn wasn't sure of what to make of it. "Maybe it's other Dwellers?"

"Out here, now? Not likely! Let's go back and tell the others!"

They hurried back down the bank and waited till they were back with Darla, Gitec and Fevol, before announcing their find.

"There is someone on the other side ahead," they were out of breath from the run, "there's a fire and the sound of laughter!"

"Where?" Gitec demanded.

"Just a little up the bank after the curve on the other side." Thiunn filled him in, "Maybe its Uncle J?"

"We better go and find out. Fevol and I will cross..."

"No. We will all go. It is Julian. I know it." Darla was so definite in her tone that there was no question. After all, sooner or later they were going to have to cross and it was very probable that the ones on the other side were Quei, Thodox and Julian.

"Okay. Be careful. Just do what we do and cross the way we cross," Fevol didn't have time to argue.

They quickly found their way to the boulders and began the crossing. Into the cool dark water they went, staying within an arms length of each other.

They could not touch bottom and eagerly reached for the slimy rocks. One by one they advanced till they all were safely across. The cool air and sound of the water made them colder than their wet clothes already made them feel.

"We'll go quietly and not reveal ourselves till we are certain of who they are," Gitec implied through his hand movements who and what he meant, "You stay behind Fevol and me." The three nodded to indicate an acceptance and understanding of the plans. With stealth they closed in upon the encampment.

As they neared, the sounds that Eruinn and Thiunn had first heard were now more clearly distinguishable though not identifiable. It was the sound of laughter and light friendly conversation. Gitec without speaking advised care and silence. They continued forward, keeping their attention on the Forest around them. Then Gitec crouched down behind a large trunk, encouraging the others to copy. They were all concealed behind trunks and the shadows created by the light of a small fire. Around the fire were three, what appeared to be, males, oblivious to their surroundings, or trunk hidden guests! Gitec gave warning looks to each inhabitant of the trunks. They all tried to see and identify the figures at the fire. One was telling a joke or a story and the others were listening...

- - - - - - - - - - - - - - - - - - -

"...I had never slept out in the woods before and was a little nervous. I kept imagining strange creatures jumping out of the woods and carrying me off," the Dwellers were amused by Julian's ability to tell the story, "There were all those childhood stories of strange creatures who lived off the flesh of youngsters. I kept looking over my shoulder and jumping at the slightest sound of movement that wasn't coming from my father or myself. Suddenly there came a..."

"Uncle J! Uncle J!" Thiunn's shouting voice, coming out of nowhere and from behind the trunk, alarmed not only Quei and Thodox, but also the others who remained hidden. Quei and Thodox jumped up scared out of their wits. Julian, upon recognizing the voice of his nephew, instantly changed from startlement to exuberance. He jumped up and stretched his arms out to his nephew.

"Thiunn!" They ran into each others arms, joyously hugged, then both spoke at the same time!

"I though we'd never see you!"

"We'd? Are Darla and Eruinn here?"

"Yes. Over there behind those trunks."

"But how...how did you know where to find me?"

By now the others had came out of hiding and the whole party turned to greeting one another before the fire. It was an unusual sight here in the Forest. Soon they all sat together and began to get caught up with the details since they had all last been together. They were not the only ones being caught up.

- - - - - - - - - - - - - - - - - - -

Merm had managed to pick up the trail of the thieves and the two dwellers just as they began the trek north to the river. There had been obstacles and sentries with Dologs sniffing here and there. Once he was out of the Dwellers' forest home the worry of discovery diminished. It was now just himself and the five ahead.

Following from a distance had been easy. The Southlanders were clumsy and noisy. It was simple for an experienced Gott to track them. They were headed in a straight path due north. By the time the five reached the river, Merm had been able to close the gap and keep them within sight. The noise and smell from the river helped to conceal his propinquity.

He watched as they crossed the river via the large boulders and waited till they were on the other side before he attempted the cross. Crossing would require that he let go of the box thereby temporarily ending its magic. He could not afford to be seen! He would cross after the five had moved on. It would not take long to catch up with them again.

- - - - - - - - - - - - - - - - - - -

Merm abhorred getting wet. No wonder the Gotts smelled so pungent. They never bathed, believing it to be unhealthy and a habit of the female from the weaker worlds! After the five had gone, he reluctantly immersed himself into the cool dark water in order to get to the boulders. Once he slipped from one of the more slimy boulders and fell back into the water No-one heard. Eventually he crossed and was standing dripping on the other side. Still no-one had noticed him!

Merm started looking for any clues to lead him and discovered on the dry forest floor, five sets of wet step marks. This was an unexpected gift. After a quick shake to remove some more of his wetness, he expeditiously continued after them. It was not long before he became aware of a loud commotion.

On hearing the voices Merm paused, found the box in his pocket, and using its magic became invisible. He then walked toward the sounds, and from a vantage point down wind, behind a large trunk, he spied upon the re-union. For now he would watch and listen. There was nothing else he could do, their numbers were too many to attempt anything. He thought of using the invisibility to creep in amongst them and find the Key, but that was too risky. It was better to wait for the right moment. It would come. Now he should gather as much information as possible and follow. The moment would come!

- - - - - - - - - - - - - - - - - - -

Darla was hugging Julian. She never really appreciated till now, how much this Stoneman meant to her.

"We were beginning to get very worried about you! Don't ever leave without saying good-bye again!"

"I'm afraid there was no other choice. There still may be no choice."

"You must complete the journey. Eruinn, Thiunn, and myself, we are here to help."

"The *Evil* is not far from us."

"Yes I've had the same feeling ever since Jard and the strangeness at Buold's."

"Their eyes are upon us. I am certain they are watching now!" Julian was pleased that Darla had similar feelings.

"Then we must not squander whatever advantage we may have." Letting go and turning to the others Darla suggested, "We should take rest here the night. One of us must always be on guard. We will take turns."

"We are more rested than you. We'll start the rotation." Quei offered on behalf of the Dwellers.

"That is kind." Darla responded.

"Thank you." Eruinn put in.

"Then let's get to bed, the sun rise is early here and we need to get to the falls. Goodnight and welcome all!" Thodox directed his comments to everyone. They all felt like a close family.

- - - - - - - - - - - - - - - - - -

Merm, who had overheard, agreed. It was time to get one last good rest. He believed that within the next sun rise there would be many changes. Changes that the party in the Forest couldn't begin to imagine!

Chapter 9.

Bad Land. What an appropriate name. Nothing would grow here. Nothing could survive here. It was just useless bad land! For as far as the eye could see, there was a sandy white cratered and ridged territory. It had to be dealt with on foot. Up and down, around obstacles and backtracking from dead ends. There was lost footing, slipping, the tedium, along with fatigue, and dark. All of this placed them in irritable moods. Not a sociable word was uttered, only an occasional cussing brought forth by the frustration of the traverse.

"How much further!" Rmont could not contain himself.

"Almost there are. Just little more," was all that Gorg answered.

The others scowled at the weakness of this Gott. Even though tired, they would prefer to drop than complain! It was a disgrace!

A shout came from one of the Riders who had been sent ahead to choose the best path and save time. "There is! Falls are."

The news was like a tonic. It rekindled the strength of the group and they hurried after the scout till they found themselves standing on the edge of the Bad Land overlooking a deep chasm. The sound and force of water was clear, but it was hidden to their sight in the darkness of the night. A path led down the side of the cliff to the water below. That, at least, was the assumption they had made.

"We down go. Camp make at bottom. We well do." Gorg was pleased that they had arrived, and had been able to show up this Gott in the process. He felt elevated in status amongst his Six.

Down into the gorge they descended, still on foot. The steepness of the path was too much to be able to ride. All around was a mist. Water was being sprayed everywhere. The roar of the crashing river, full of whirlpools and rocks, was deafening. By the time they all reached the bottom, they were drenched! They stood in front of the fast moving rapids and one of the multiple, Falls of Light. Rmont understood why the falls were so named. The water seemed to glisten with a luminosity of its own. There were probably 'glow rocks' scattered beneath its depths. That was his only explanation.

The place where they had stopped was near the river. To their left and stretching high up, were a series of cascading waterfalls. Over to the extreme right, forming a semi-circular shape, was the other end of the falls. They were outstanding! Being dark, it was not possible to see more detail, but the path, as they would discover in the sun rise, led on till it ended right into the left hand side of one powerful Fall.

To the right of their position, and behind, was a sheltered area which had been created over the eons by the watery erosion into the rock cliff wall. A large overhanging rock roof, precarious in appearance, would provide a dryer resting place for the seven to make camp.

"We there camp make. In sun rise we more learn." Gorg motioned his Six to break for camp. Each Rider had a duty and within a very short time, a large canopy was assembled and they were all sitting around one Rider, who was trying to start a fire from the damp driftwood.

Rmont was impressed at the efficiency of the assembling of the camp. He walked over under the natural roof and toward the canopy: "Here this will help." He presented a Gott light stick to the Rider who was trying to start the fire. One pull of its igniting ribbon and it would supply light or heat, or act as a catalyst in starting a blaze.

"Thanks," said the Rider timidly, as he took the stick. It was formality, a begrudged nicety that was proffered to those allies not of the Kith.

Rmont remained and watched as the stick was set aflame and tossed into the driftwood by the Rider. Gradually it caught and the other watching Riders prepared to add more wood, creating and fueling a huge bonfire. He would be happy to be away from these childish oafs. He sighed and wondered at what he was doing here in such a horrid place. *Had Merm realized what was going on and started to make his way to Tika?* This was the only known pass. Was he too early? Was he too late? What should he do next? All these questions plagued him as he tried to warm his body and dry his dampness from the now steadily growing bonfire. What he urgently needed was sleep. In the sun rise he would attempt to find some answers.

Gorg, who was observing Rmont, came up, "What wrong is?"

"Nothing. Just tired."

"Things better be."

"I was just wondering what we will do next."

"Find what we search."

"Yes but how, where?"

"Too much questions ask. Now sleep. In sun rise we see." Gorg wasn't much for pondering thought. "You sleep there. In sun rise talk more."

Rmont, guided by Gorg, found his pebbled bed under the canopy close to the cliff wall. It was quieter here, like climbing into a shell of the great oceans. One of the Riders was put in charge of his mount, so there was nothing left to concern him. He lay down, curled up and fell into deep sleep.

With Rmont out of the way Gorg turned to the other Six who were still awake and sitting under the rock canopy by the large fire. "This Gott not good. No trust. Come find, now not know."

"What do now?" Tan was curious. Now that they were at the Falls of Light, in which direction were they to go?

"Go Tika. Old city powerful is. There find what Gott want."

"Know you way?"

"Gott know. He show." Gorg wasn't worried about the direction. There wasn't a destination to which a Rider couldn't find his way.

"Weak this one is." Tan spoke as the others sipped drink, "How Gotts so strong and feared?"

"Many Troop there are. Large and mean. Good in many not few!" They chuckled after Gorg made this comment which was considered amongst the Kith as an insult. "Much gain will come. We watch and wait. No trust this Gott. You keep eye on."

- - - - - - - - - - - - - - - - - -

"But Wakan, I do not understand how they were able to travel so far! I had the Southlander in my grip. He was gone. There was no more struggle left!"

"They are near the city! Once they are passed the falls it will be very difficult for any of us to intervene. They must be stopped! We are *forbidden* to cross!"

"It will be done. They will not enter the zone. The Key will not be returned to Tika."

"This will be our last chance. There is no more need to hide. They are certainly aware of us now. Use all the power you can to stop them." As Wakan's image faded, Dorluc spoke after him.

"Yes. You are correct. The drain in the Magic is very strong now. They grow more awake."

Dorluc had not discovered the survival of Julian until he had returned to the view screen and it was displaying the party of eight around the camp fire. It did not reveal the invisible Merm. Dorluc was horrified!

They were headed to Tika. Once they passed the Falls of Light, they would be protected from his direct influence, by the zone of Tika. The zone exposed powerful magic which could be accessed and used by any of knowledge. This additional 'charging' would make the Southlanders a formidable force! It would then require all the energy and skill that the *Evil* could muster just to equal the strength.

Dorluc would try one last influence of Merm, before he made known his existence again. The episode in Jard against the youngster was foolish. He had not been prepared for the rebuttal. If the female had not been present, the outcome would have been different. Now that the youngsters were close to the zone, it would be difficult to attempt any similar surprise as the one in Jard!

Dorluc changed his attention to Merm. He closed his eyes and searched his thoughts. It was a sensing, a feeling of a presence; one that he knew well after all this time of influencing Merm.

- - - - - - - - - - - - - - - -

Merm was still in the Forest. After hearing the conversation of the re-union, he considered it wise to move to a more concealing resting place, a place where he would not have to worry about becoming visible once he fell to sleep and let go of his grip upon the box! How wearing all this had been! He wandered farther up the riverbank and discovered a cave-like site amongst the rocks and tree stumps. He had no thought of other slithery creatures that might inhabit there. The Gotts had a thick skin! Making himself as comfortable as he could in his dampness, he propped himself up against the stump in the back of the shelter. After placing the box back into the pocket from which it had come, he took a last look at his surroundings and when he was satisfied, closed his eyes and dozed off.

- - - - - - - - - - - - - - - - - -

Dorluc located Merm in his mind. His actual physical location was unknown, but his condition was one of sleep! How fortunate, there would be no time wasted waiting for the dream state and another final influencing. Dorluc focused his power on Merm. He did not require any help this time, as Merm by now would be very receptive to Dorluc's control.

Merm tossed as Dorluc entered his dreams. Again there was the blue opaqueness, but this time the figure that came to Merm's mind was more distinguishable.

"The thieves are escaping." Dorluc started directly. "They are not stopped. Soon they will be unstoppable."

"They are strong in number now."

"Yes, but I am not speaking of their number. They are awakening to the great Magic of the Key. They will use this power to dominate the worlds. You will be the first. They are in the northern Forest approaching the Falls of Light."

"Yes. I am with them."

"With them?!"

"Yes I have followed them and used the magic of the box of the Key. I am near them now, but their numbers are too many for me alone to stop them."

"I will give you strength and the knowledge to combat them. You will have the magic of thoughts. You will be able to create illusion that will intimidate and slow them."

"But how will I learn the use of this magic?"

"Whatever is in your thought, you will be able to project upon them. Use your thoughts and concentrate. You will remember all of this after you awaken."

"If it is only illusion, how can I confront and stop them?"

"Only you will know that the image is not real. They will believe it to be real. That will be your advantage. You must get to the Falls of Light and stop them from crossing into the zone of Tika."

"How will I find the way?"

"You will know by use of your magic. I have given you the knowledge of passing. You will be admitted by the knowledge of the Old Ones that I will place into your being now. Follow the direction your thoughts take. The Key must not pass to the inner obelisk of Tika. You *must* prevent that outcome. Once it finds its place in the obelisk, its magic will be lost to the thieves. I will not be able to go there. You will be alone against them all!"

"There are others on the way to Tika who are ahead and can help. They will be able to entrap the thieves before the crossing!" Yes, Rmont will be a saving grace again! Merm was feeling a more comfortable joining with Dorluc and was pleased at his timing to send out Rmont to solicit the Riders to the cause.

"When you awake, start for the falls. I will speak with those already there. Do not let them pass over. You must not let the Key return to Tika!"

Dorluc faded out of Merm's dream. He would now locate those at the falls. Merm would sleep on till sun rise, then remembering all, would continue to the Falls of Light. He would feel renewed and more powerful. The greed for the Magic was dominating. He did not and would not question the image of his dreams. He trusted them. This was all part of Dorluc's influence. If the thieves crossed into the zone, that influence would gradually wane. Once Merm was free of it, he may not be as cooperative. The Lord of the Gotts would realize that other motivations and goals, different from his, existed, and would enslave him forever. This fact of life was prompting Dorluc to complete his repossession of the Key and the power of the *Passwords*, before that occurred!

Merm tossed in his shelter after Dorluc's powerful sway had let go. He rolled over onto his side still asleep, but no longer dreaming.

- - - - - - - - - - - - - - - - - -

Dorluc concentrated again. He put his thoughts to the Falls of Light. His spirit drifted there, and hovered above the encampment of the Riders. It hovered, while Dorluc determined which of the seven he should influence. Spying the sole sleeping Gott, he surmised that this must be the one of whom Merm had spoken. His spirit existence hovered over this large Gott; Dorluc spoke telepathically to Rmont. Rmont, in his sleep, heard a voice. He awoke and was startled to see the blue opaque image over top.

"What are you!" Rmont spoke loudly causing Dorluc to hush him.

"Do not talk. We will speak through our thoughts." Rmont closed his mouth and was amazed that he was able to hear and speak without uttering a sound. "What are you?" he reiterated.

"I have come from Merm."

"The Lord Merm of the Gotts?"

"Yes. He is close and soon will be here. He has sent me to warn of the thieves."

"Thieves?" Rmont was testing.

"Those who took the Key! They are also headed this way. They must not cross the river."

"That shouldn't be a problem."

"Do not underestimate their strength. They are of great magic. Do not let them pass. Hold them till Merm arrives. He is not long behind them."

"I will tell the Riders ..."

"Do not speak of our conversation with them. They are not to be trusted," Dorluc did not want any more awareness of his existence than necessary. "Prepare them for the thieves, but make no mention of Merm or myself."

"Who are you?"

"I am a friend. One who has helped before. My name is of no consequence. You must not let the thieves pass!"

Rmont thought on these last words. There had been many times in the past when he had wondered at the

ability of Merm and himself to overcome obstacles
that seemed so impossible. He wondered at the visions that Merm had often spoken of, and then realized. Perhaps Merm had a strange powerful ally. He
recalled the episode at Norkleau in which all had considered Merm dead, and then accepting this entity, he
said: "I will do as you ask." All the times of trial and
tribulation were starting to make sense to Rmont.

"In the sun rise prepare. They will soon arrive."
Dorluc's voice lingered as he disappeared before
Rmont's eyes.

Rmont was shaken, but resolved to do as he was
asked by this strange force. He had learned over time
that certain things were better not questioned. This
was one of those times. He had been entrusted to retrieve the Key from the thieves. The intervention of
this 'thing' made it easier to accomplish. The sooner
they were captured, the sooner he would be able to
return to Aug.

The journey here had been hard. He did not like the
idea of continuing on through this rough terrain to
Tika. If he was smart and used the Riders properly,
the whole quest could end here and now. In the sun
rise he would organize the Riders. For the rest of the
night, Rmont would make his plan. He was now even
more confident of the success of Merm and himself,
after the conversation with the image. The loss of the
fight with the South had only been a battle, not the
war!

- - - - - - - - - - - - - - - - - - - -

Dorluc composed himself. He was watching the
view screen. He had done what he could for the moment. All he could do now, was watch and wait! The
darkness of the eve was still intense, and the view
screen was not making the great jumps from scene to
scene as it had done before. The fluctuations were all

centered upon the northern area of the Burning Forest. This was the area where all the drain to the Magic was now concentrated. There was also an indication of a newer source of drain far to the north in the vicinity of Tika. It was a weak one, but it was steadily increasing.

Dorluc began to reminisce about the Old Ones, and the corporeal life he had known. How he longed to be physical again. He missed the tactileness of existence. If only he had not been discovered in his attempt to use the Password for his own gain! By now he would have learned much more about the Magic and risen to greater power. But he had been caught, along with his followers and punished. The ancient anger against his punishers swelled within him. He must control it! In the first times of his banishment, he had almost gone crazy from the depravation of the senses. It was only due to his mastery and skill within the Magic, that he had been able to withstand the tremendous pressure that loss created. He also began to fixate on finding a way to reverse his condition. It had taken ages, but he found the way: the *Passwords of Promise*. There was also the ancient Key that would unlock these secrets of the Old Ones, his very own compatriots, who had hidden away the great wealth of knowledge acquired by them in order to preserve the Balance. Dorluc was aware that such knowledge had once existed, but thought it had been all lost, long ago. The discovery of the Key, first by Ho and now Merm, was the final realization that all the time of searching for a missing link, which could provide him the necessary magic to return to the living, was now nearing fruition.

- - - - - - - - - - - - - - - - - -

When Merm awoke the sun had long ago risen. In the panic that he had overslept, giving the thieves a head start, he jumped up and hit his head upon a tree stump of his shelter. He caught himself before calling out the pain. As he was still visible, he rummaged through his pocket until he grabbed the box. Before initiating its magic, he found himself recalling the strange dream of his sleep. He remembered gradually the details: the power, and the need to stop the thieves before crossing at the Falls of Light. He wasn't certain whether or not to believe, so he tried to test the dream.

He concentrated his thought on his favorite meal, he was very hungry, and before him appeared a table full of the best delicacies. He tried other items and one by one they materialized. Each time he attempted to touch, his hand passed right through, as if they were not there and in fact they were not! So the dream was true. He had new magic! Having convinced himself, he touched the box and forgot about his thoughts. Instantly the items disappeared along with him.

Merm made his way carefully to the place where the thieves had encamped for the night. They were gone! Only smoldering slag was left where their fire had been. They must have left early in the sun rise. There was a freshly trodden path leading off northward. Merm decided to follow and remain invisible until he could ascertain exactly where they were. He did not wish to be seen. He remembered what had been said in the dream about warning Rmont at the falls. This made him calmer. At least the thieves would be expected and held until he arrived himself. He hurried off in the direction that led to the Falls of Light.

For most of the trip a small Forest of sparsely placed trees was his scenery. It was beautiful, then abruptly it ended and he faced the ordeal of the Bad Land. It was hot and dry. Seeing no more trace of the thieves, he embarked by instinct on his own path through this wasteland. He was hungry and thirsty, but he knew he would make it through without either of these being satisfied. The thought of Rmont catching the thieves energized him. There would be food and drink enough on the other side of the Bad Land.

- - - - - - - - - - - - - - - - - - -

Rmont had awakened the Riders early, before the sun rise. He did not want to chance not being ready for the guests. When Gorg questioned him on how he was so sure that the thieves were coming this way and had not already passed, he merely hardened his tone and said, "Did I question the wisdom of the Head Rider when he pushed us on after the Forest? Did I question when you told us to go down this gorge? No, and all was the way it should be. You knew well the right things to do. There was no reason. There is no reason now! I know the right things to do. Do not question these things. The thieves will come and we must be ready to surprise and stop them!"

Gorg and his Six understood the logic of Rmont's thinking. He was right of course. It was their job to get Rmont here to the Falls of Light and it was Rmont's job to take care of the thieves. Each had their own tasks. Each had there own expertise!

Rmont placed each of the Riders in their position to await the arrival of those with the valuable. They were to wait until the thieves were well into the gorge and on their way along the path toward the falls before they ambushed them. It was simple. Nothing could go wrong. Even a Rider could do it!

Rmont had half expected their guests to arrive by mid sun. The mid sun came and went. The Riders were beginning to grow impatient and doubt his competence. Gorg came out of his hiding and down the path to Rmont. The others observed and were quietly making fun of the Gott.

"No thiefs is. Too long wait. Maybe nother way go!?" Gorg was speaking loud enough so all could hear.

Though he was himself uncertain, Rmont did not show it in his answer, " They will be here soon. You should be in your place. When they are at the top of the cliff it will be too late for you to get back to your spot."

"In spot already too much. Tired am of this!" Gorg was impatient and was now challenging Rmont's decisions and position. This was the way of the Kith.

"Get back to your position..."

"Come does!" A loud whisper came through the ranks, Rider to Rider, until it had reached all. Gorg was embarrassed that he had been wrong and Rmont right. He quickly turned and ran like a fool to return to his position. The other Riders empathized with their Head Rider's predicament.

All eyes turned to the top of the cliff. The noise from the falls concealed any noises made by either parties. Just as Gorg was back in place, the first of the thieves appeared at the top. He began to move down into the gorge after a paused moment of taking in the incredible sight. They all waited for the next thief, but no one followed. Rmont wondered if this thief was just the one in the lead, or a scout making sure all was clear before the rest entered the fissure created by the powerful Pass River amongst the rock. The lone figure came deeper into their midst. It was becoming obvious that there were not any others. The hidden Riders all looked to Gorg and Rmont for direction. Rmont indicated to wait a little longer and then strike!

The figure was coming closer and closer. It was large and familiar. What was going on? Then out of their hiding jumped the Riders. The thief was caught and held by two. He was a strong fellow. He struggled and swung at whatever he could. The Riders swung back and kicked him. They began to enjoy the catch. The thief was obviously becoming hurt.

Rmont jumped from his hiding and ran to the scrummage. He was yelling out to the Riders to hold. They did not listen. As he got closer he realized that the thief was a Gott! "Hold on there!" he yelled again.

"Rmont! Rmont is that you? Get these oafs off of me!"

"My Lord! How..."

"Get them off!" Merm was furious.

The Riders began to see that this was not who they all thought it might be. It was humorous, but they tried to hide their laughter. It was the Lord of the Gotts. He was not liked by them, and they each tried one more jab under the pretense that they thought he was the thief and had not heard Rmont!

Rmont burrowed into the mess and helped his bruised Lord to his feet. "My Lord. How are you here before the thieves? This is a great mistake."

Mistake indeed. Gorg and his Six were now standing together meekly. Gorg was re-established in his status. The Gotts deserved the mess into which they had put themselves. A Rider would not have made such an error!

As Merm rose, Rmont was brushing off the dirt from the 'ambush'.

"Stop that you fool! Didn't you see that I was a Gott? Where are the thieves? They were ahead of me and should have been here first!"

"We have been waiting since sun rise and you are the only one to come down into the gorge. No one else has appeared."

"Impossible! They must have come this way. It is the only way to cross the river."

"Maybe there is another way, one that we do not know?"

"What are you saying! Do you think me a idiot?!"

"No my Lord never! It is just that many strange things have happened here, voices that don't speak and images in the night!"

"So he did come. He came to warn you of the thieves?"

"Yes, but who or what is he?"

"He is a friend. Trust him. He is helping us stop the thieves," Merm saw that the Riders were overhearing, "Now let's go down and revise our plans."

Merm and Rmont continued the walk to the bottom, Gorg and his Riders followed. When they were all on the flat near the river beneath the falls, Merm addressed them all.

"It is good to see that the Riders are so efficient," it was said in humor and they snickered, "Perhaps we can now, after that practice, catch the real thieves. They will be here."

"What if no come?" Gorg showed deference to his employer.

"We will wait till the eve, if they do not come this way we will assume that they have found another route. We will continue on through the falls."

"How we that do?"

"The path leads to an entrance under the falls," he pointed out the path that went along the river and ended on the left side in the falls. Nobody had yet thought to check that route, being so obvious in its brutal end. They were wrong, "the path continues under the falls. There is a way through. A doorway of stone. I know the way to open that passage." Dorluc in the dreams, had given his old knowledge of the pass tune. With it three would be able to pass. "Only three may pass. The rest will wait behind for our return and also keep a watch for the thieves in case they do eventually arrive."

"I go," Gorg volunteered and spoke to his Six, "Tan in charge is, while gone!"

"Good," Merm was going to choose Gorg anyway, "Rmont will be the third! Gorg, it would be wise to place two Riders above to forewarn us of any sighting of the thieves. We don't want to be caught by surprise again!"

"Yes. Two go," Gorg picked two out and gave them their orders, "When see anything, here come fast!"

"Now, can you offer me some food and drink?"

"Certainly Lord. It is over here."

They all walked back to the sheltered area. The mist from the falls was still heavy and they were once again becoming drenched.

"I don't understand Lord, if this is the only place to pass, how is it that they have not yet arrived?" Rmont spoke as he prepared food.

Merm was sitting on a rock, Gorg and his remaining Riders were nearby preparing their own refreshments.

"It is odd. There is no explanation that I can offer. This is the only way to cross over. I know this from our friend. They *were* ahead of me!"

"Could they have become aware of you and tried another strategy?"

"No. They were not aware of my presence after the Dwellers' home in the forest."

"You found the secret of those of the Burning Forest?"

"Yes. They are not the creatures told of in our stories. They are simple woodsmen, hiding away. They are very aware of us, though we ignorant, of them. When this is over, we will send a Troop in after them."

"So they are helping the thieves?"

"It would seem so."

"Then perhaps they know of another pass and have taken them that way."

"That is doubtful. There is only this one way. It is the safest and most direct. Any other would be too arduous and slow. As the thieves are in a hurry and worried about our pursuit, they would choose the fastest way."

"How are you certain they are concerned?"

"This is the help I am getting from our 'friend'.

They both fell silent as Rmont presented his Lord with a plate full of food and a cup of drink.

Dorluc who had been watching and witnessed the mistake, tried to understand what had happened. He set the view screen to discover the whereabouts of the party of thieves. It was not able to find a trace of them! Something had happened, but what? He knew of only the one way to cross the river in order to reach Tika. The door under the falls was well hidden and would only open for those who knew the proper tune. It was a melody the Old Ones had kept secret to their own kind. As Dorluc was once one of them, he still remembered the sounds. The melody was not changed, because from the place where Dorluc had been banished, he would not be able to have any type of physical contact nor involvement. The Old Ones had not foreseen this possibility, or had they?

Dorluc remained in front of the view screen still flustered by the disappearance of the thieves. This was yet another delay tactic somehow foolishly overlooked by him and caused by the Magic of his punishers. Even though they were gone, their presence and Magic was still strong! He had been sloppy in underestimating their presence. He would be more careful from now on.

Chapter 10.

Fevol had been the last watch and as a result was still awake whilst the others were still sleeping. Before getting them up, he spent a few moments checking over the area. There was something very odd in the air, but he was not able to put his finger on

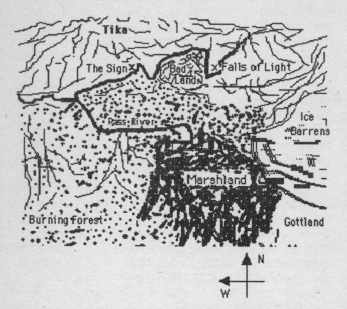

Map of the Far North Around Tika

it. The Forest was quieter than usual and more vacant

than usual. This was always an omen of some disorder! Not being successful in any type of discovery, he awoke the other Dwellers first. After he expressed his concerns, they too agreed that there was something out of the ordinary and it was close by.

"It might be wiser to take the longer route to the Falls of Light," Gitec suggested.

"Yes. If that Gott is following, it will be harder for him to travel alone through the river cliffs and gorge." Fevol recalled the episode at Buold's and considered the possibility of the Gott still being out there and keeping close behind.

"Yes it will be harsher and longer, but safer if we are being watched. It will be impossible for anyone to follow along without being spotted by us from ahead. They would be easily seen by us in the distance Let's wake the others and get underway." Quei was back in command, being the most senior amongst them.

One by one they awakened the Southworlders, explaining to each the necessity to take the longer route due north to the river and follow the gorge to the falls. They would avoid the Bad Land and keep to the gorge till they reached the top of the falls. Everyone agreed it was the most sensible path to take.

By mid sun they had met the river. The Forest had become sparser till finally there was only the cratered earth and cliffs which meandered their way into and down to the deep crevice that had been eroded over time by the Pass river. Beyond was a canyon that stretched as far as they could see. On their side the land just ended and fell to the watery depths below.

It was impossible to cross at any point. The river was too fast and strong; its rapids lethal. The gorge was too deep to attempt a climb, even if you did survive the crossing. They would follow the gorge from atop on their side as long as they were able. The sight was humbling.

As they each made their way along the ridge, Darla,

Eruinn and Thiunn began to feel as if they had been here before. They had, but they hadn't. Darla noted that the stones in Jewel were still glowing and were slightly brighter. It would seem that Jewel also felt a familiarity. Clearly they were very close to the origin of all; the beginning place, the source from which their awakening moles had come. The further along the ridge they progressed, the more certain each of the Chosen Ones were as to their destination. The Dwellers were not changing, only Julian and the three. Together they began to feel a merging strength and unity. It was of great age.

Julian was uneasy. There was something more he knew, but what? He remembered the voice amongst the Moonfruit; he remembered the words of Buold: *there was a sign that only those chosen will know.* What did it all mean? He gave up trying to understand and kept walking forward with the unconscious sureness that all was as it should be. The panic and fear of the *Evil* was diminishing. He could not explain why. He turned to comment but Darla spoke first.

"Yes. We all feel it. This is home. We have all traveled this ridge before. Do not be alarmed. There are still many questions within each of us. There, look at Eruinn and Thiunn," she subtly drew Julian's attention to them as they walked ahead, "They also seem more relaxed and self assured."

"Do you believe that we have all shared in this at some earlier time?"

"Yes. The dormant essence within each of us has been linked for generations. All the experiences and feelings of those times are deep within and rising up into our present lives in order to assist us in our tasks."

"Will we ever be the same again?"

"Better," was all that she said, before they fell to silence once more.

They walked all the afternoon. The canyons becoming older and deeper. The river below deep and powerful. Quei who had been at the lead of the party stopped and waited for them all to catch up. As he waited, there was no sense that anyone or anything had been following or watching. His keen forest sense was right. For the danger was ahead waiting at the Falls of Light. At this rate they would arrive there at the beginning of the sun setting.

"Let's stop awhile and rest. The last leg of the journey is here," they all welcomed Quei's suggestion.

They sat on some rocks near the edge of the ridge overlooking the canyons and river. It was as if the place was a natural 'rest vista'. The cliffs of the canyon had risen up through ages of erosion. An erosion that had sculpted them into eerie disproportionate shapes. Eruinn and Thiunn played games trying to imagine what the other saw in the variety of shapes surrounding them. This humored the rest of the party.

Julian, admiring their innocence and calm, joined them. He sat next to Eruinn and gazed out over what was almost an abyss. He looked northward through the cliff tops. His eyes began to settle on one cliff. There was something different about this one. It was four or five cliffs away on the north west side. Its shape was like the head and beak of a bird. He scrutinized it.

"What are you looking at Uncle J?" Thiunn was drawn by his Uncle's vacant gaze.

"What..." Thiunn's voice broke his trance. "Look, over there," he pointed out the spot, "what do you see?"

Thiunn and now an interested Eruinn, who thought that his Uncle was playing along with them, joined in.

"Do you see a beak of a bird pointing to the east side of the canyon?"

"You're not meant to give it away so soon, Uncle J. That's not the way the game is played!" Eruinn was annoyed.

"I'm not playing a game. Look over there. What do you see?"

They both scanned the horizon, scrutinizing each peak. One, two, nothing but scragged cliffs. Four, five...five was different.

"Yes. It does seem different from the others. Look." Eruinn helped Thiunn.

"I see it too! Not so much a beak, but more a finger, and it's pointing to there," Thiunn raised his own finger indicating an imaginary line that led to a place on their side of the canyon, about a thousand lengths ahead, "over there!"

"It is the way to Tika. I know it. You tell the others while Thiunn and I go ahead," Julian seemed possessed. This was the *something else*. This was the sign that Buold had foretold; the place that only the Chosen would know. From deep inside, as he rushed toward the spot, he did understand!

As Julian and Thiunn were leaving, Eruinn ran to Darla and the Dwellers encouraging them to hurry, "Uncle Julian has found the way. Hurry!" He picked up his brother's things and went.

"What was all that about?" Just as Quei was getting used to these Southworlders something odd happened.

"We'd better get going. Julian must have found something important," Darla answered as she rose, picked up her gear; also a small bag that Julian in his hurry had left behind, and started after the others without waiting for the Dwellers' decision.

Julian was standing with Thiunn near the edge of the cliff. There were several large boulders and over the edge a narrow ledge running about six lengths to where another part of the cliff jutted out. On the other side was the sign and it was pointing to these boulders.

"What do you think Uncle J?" Thiunn was stumped. He half hoped on the way that there would be some magical entrance sitting in the middle of this arid place.

Julian considered. There was a gnawing inside him,

a recognition. He knew the way. He knew the answer, but what was it. He offhandledly blurted out, "Down there!"

"You mean the river?!"

"No there, the ledge. What we want is there."

"Are you sure? Its pretty tricky to be climbing over these crumbling cliffs. The ledge may not support the weight!"

As if he hadn't heard he blurted out a command, "Here give me a hand and hold onto my belt." Julian went to his hands and knees and carefully looked over the cliff edge. It was an incredible sight. The cliff walls were rough and hard; thousands of lengths below ran the river. If you were to fall...he chose not to visualize the thought! He tried to lower himself toward the ledge just below him, but it would be impossible head first. He stopped and turned around so that he could attempt to go down feet first. By now Thiunn had changed his grip from the belt and was now helping lower Julian down by keeping a secure hold of one of his uncle's outstretched hands. Julian slowly worked his way down. The ledge below was still another length beyond his presently secured reach and stretched grasp of Thiunn on the upper ridge. He would have to let go and risk the danger of dropping and falling from the ledge.

"Wait Uncle J! Don't!" Thiunn was too late in his anticipation of his uncle's actions. Julian was descending the cliff wall all by himself. He slowly went down without the added safety of Thiunn's grasp. Thiunn crawled forward and lying on the ground extended his hands to try and help his Uncle's decent. Julian returned a warm smile.

"I knew I could count on you. When I get down, keep me in sight."

"Please be careful."

"I haven't come this far to..." Julian lost his footing. Thiunn took up the sudden surge of weight, but it was too much for him. He slowly was being dragged after his falling Uncle. His arms went over the edge still gripped on to Julian. Then the fall stopped. Julian felt the solidness of the ledge. "Its okay. I'm on the ledge!"

"That was close." Thiunn let go and watched as Julian secured his position in his mind and began to move along the ledge, hugging the cliff wall. "Don't look down Uncle J!"

Julian hated heights. He realized that a look down would pull him over. He kept his mind on his goal and talked out loud to distract himself.

About this time, Eruinn then Darla arrived at the edge.

"Where is he?" they both panicked.

"Down there." Thiunn's answer confused them.

"How?..." Eruinn couldn't believe that Julian was gone!

Thiunn caught on, "No, he's down there on a ledge. He climbed down. He's alright!"

On hearing the three above, Julian jokingly called out: "What are you waiting for, come on down!"

Darla leaned over, "We'll wait to see what happens to you first, if you don't mind! Now what are you doing down there?"

Julian reached the end of the ledge. A solid wall was in front of him. He placed one hand upon it and brushed away.

"What is it?" Eruinn spoke what the others were thinking.

"Remember Aug and the tunnel entrance."

"Yes."

"That's what this is. Yes, here it is." Julian had found the symbol carved into the cliff. It was the same as the others he had encountered before, in placement and design. Finding the raised impressions he pushed them simultaneously as he had done in the passageway before. The melody, similar to the other entrance in Aug, sounded and after a loud squeaking, a doorway opened inward. It was just large enough to let him pass through. He entered.

The three above were amazed. How had Julian known? They understood as soon as they had posed the thought.—This was the secret entrance which led to Tika! There was no need to cross at the Falls of Light!

The Dwellers arrived out of breath, just as Thiunn was being lowered to the ledge. "What's going on?" Quei shouted when he noticed no Julian, and Thiunn being dropped over the cliff.

"Julian has found another way to Tika. We must go. It is the only way to escape the *Evil* and Merm. He will not be able to follow after we are gone. Quickly. We will help you down." Darla explained further, thinking the Dwellers wanted to come.

"No. We are not permitted. Buold has ordered us not to cross onto the path to Tika. We will return to the Tribe." Quei gave Darla some rope and a few supplies that were in the small bag he carried, "May the power of Three be upon you. We hope to see you again."

Each of the Dwellers said their good-byes and then helped lower Eruinn and Darla down. They watched as the last one disappeared behind the closing cliff door.

Inside the dark passageway, Darla held Jewel up to illuminate the dark. Eruinn, Thiunn and Julian were all within an arms length or two of each other. "Here Julian, hold Jewel while I get the illuminator from my bag." Julian grasped it without question, pleased to have control of the light.

It was a tiny narrow passageway, very plain. The light from Jewel's stones was multi-colored and made it hard to make anything out, but it was light!

"Oah...there it is." Darla pulled out the oblong stone that cast off a light large enough to see a few lengths in every direction.

The air was still and old. They were all standing in

a long tunnel with only one way to proceed.

"After you Julian," Julian frowned at Darla's invitation. He was in the lead and exchanged Jewel for the illuminator. They began a very conservative movement along the tunnel. The nephews were in the middle, Darla at the rear.

It wasn't more that ten lengths when Julian found himself at the beginning of a tiny steep staircase. It was all hand cut from the inside cliff rock.

"Looks like we are going down. There are stairs here. Be careful, they are very steep," Julian started in the downward direction.

It was very small. The steps were cut out of and passed through the cliff. The tunnel narrowed so that each of them instinctively put their arms out with hands running along the smooth cool rock, for support. Their center of balance was off. These were not the type of stairs to be foolish upon! The descent was steep. If one were to slip, they would probably not have been able to recover, and would continue the slide to wherever the end of these went!

An eternity passed and claustrophobic terror was settling in. Coupled with the old air within this passage, the travelers were tiring from their efforts. It was getting hot and close.

"There's a left turn ahead," Julian informed, breaking the monotony.

The tunnel became less steep and abruptly turned ninety degrees to their left. It continued to slope slightly down. They kept going.

"The rock is getting moist here." Julian's hand was wet.

"We're going under the river." Darla shouted from behind.

"I hope it doesn't spring a leak under here," Eruinn was right. There was no hope of surviving a flooding from the river above.

"I wonder how they made this tunnel?" Thiunn marveled at the feat of engineering, "They sure knew what they were doing!"

They kept walking. Soon their feet were stepping through tiny puddles caused by the condensation on the rock that was dripping over their heads. Their apprehension heightened. Were they going to find the other side and get out from under here?

The tunnel steps began to slope up. Soon they were in a dry tunnel again with a set of stairs as steep as the downward climb, but going up. Though fatigued they persevered. In about a fifth of the time it had taken them to reach the abrupt turn from their surface descent, the stairs ended. The tunnel opened up and they found themselves in a large cavernous room. It was alight with the same plants that had illuminated the Palace under the Stars!

"Wow! This is incredible. Imagine how long this place has been this way!" Eruinn noted the obvious.

"The passage probably continues over there on the other side of the cavern." Thiunn recognized the layout of this type of room. As with the other ones that he had seen on the way to Norkleau, there were many intricate etchings upon every clear piece of rock. The symbols were of the same type as before and it seemed logical then that the overall design would also be the same.

"Maybe we should rest here before going on. It will be safe and who knows when we'll have the luxury to relax again! It can't be more than half a sun rise to Tika. We could stay here and reach Tika by the next mid sun."

"Thiunn is right and we do need the rest."

"Alright you two. Let's set up over there." Julian pointed to the far corner, it just seemed like the right spot!

The cavern was huge. Much larger than any other one that they had seen. The light from the plants was constant and a hint of green in color, making it easy for them to find their way over and put their things together in one place, just in case they needed to leave in a hurry. After settling in, each ate some of the rations that the Dwellers had given them before entering the tunnel. They were safe for now and almost at their destination. The chance to sleep peacefully was welcomed.

"Darla," Julian was lying down ready to sleep, "Thank you."

- - - - - - - - - - - - - - - - - -

"Thieves come not!" Gorg was tired of waiting. It was time to be more offensive in their strategies.

Merm was both angry and bewildered. The image of his dreams was never wrong. There must be some misunderstanding. What should he do? Wait longer to see if they arrived? Go back and try to find them? Or move ahead and cross the river? The image stressed the importance of not letting the thieves pass, but what if they already had and were now near their destination? Then what would happen to the Key? There were so many questions and possibilities. Gorg's forwardness was an irritation at the wrong time.

"Shut up! Let me think!" Merm considered his options.

"No tell shut up!" Gorg was tired, and had had enough of these Gotts.

Merm turned his new magic upon him. To the astonishment of Rmont, as well as the other Riders, a very large and ugly beast materialized and threatened Gorg.

"If you don't shut up now, this creature will deal with you and the rest! Any complaints!"

"No complain. Stop beast. Lord of Gotts powerful is!"

With a change of Merm's thought the creature vanished. Gorg backed away with new respect. Rmont did not utter a word.

"It is time to go on. If they have already crossed, we

will catch up with them, if they haven't they will eventually catch up with us. Either way, we must get to Tika and reclaim the Key! Rmont, bring some supplies...and that," he meant Gorg, "We will cross over at the end of the path."

Rmont gathered the few things they would need and called Gorg to accompany him and Merm up the path that led into the left side of the falls. The other Riders were ordered to remain in camp until their return— whenever that might be! After Merm's display of magic, they obeyed without further complaint.

The three marched on foot up the path. They came to its end, to go any further required passing through the thundering water. Gorg and Rmont wondered if Merm really knew what he was doing. Was he right that there was another side under the falls and not just a void that would wash them off the edge of the path, and into the whirlpools below? There was no choice.

"I will walk through first, then you follow. Just keep going straight. You will be safe. If you wander from a straight line you will end up down below!" Merm then walked right into the falling water and was gone.

Nervously, Rmont, after a few moments followed. Gorg was left standing alone. If he did not follow he would lose status amongst his Six. They would not respect a coward. Also if he did not follow there would be no reward and all his time and efforts wasted. He only had one option. Taking hold of himself, he walked straight into the falls.

The water pounded upon each of them as they walked. Its force almost overpowering. They walked. Water was everywhere along with the thunder of the falls. It was difficult to see a thing. They just kept to the straight path that was in their mind. Five paces and still not through. Six, maybe Merm was wrong! Nine—and they were through!

Merm was waiting with a smile as they cleared the falls and wiped the water from their faces. "Here it is.

Come over to this wall."

The noise under the falls was intense. Anything said had to be yelled out. Rmont and Gorg came over to Merm. There was nothing but a thin ledge and a symbol on the wall.

"Now what? Where door?" Gorg was careful not to offend the Lord Merm.

In his dream, Dorluc had imparted the knowledge that might be needed by Merm. To open the passage required this special knowledge. Only those of Tika knew the way. Those who were not of Tika would not be given passage through the falls.

Merm concentrated upon the symbol on the wall. He raised his hand toward it and depressed three of the four buttons simultaneously. A melody sounded and after a squeaking a space in the wall opened inward. The entrance of the Chosen, was now available to these three. Merm smiled and beckoned them in. It was dark inside, so Rmont lit a hand torch that was taken from his bag. It was a little damp from the crossing, but he did manage to set it aflame. The rock door closed, taking with it the noise of the falls.

They stood quietly together as Rmont held the torch in different directions, so they could better see where they were. It was a cave, probably eroded naturally and existing before the ancient times. A path was visible to the right.

"There we are. We will take that path. We will keep only one torch alight at a time. It can't be too far away. Remember, Rmont, what happened in the tunnel at Norkleau. We don't want to lose anyone here!"

"Yes my Lord. If we stay together it should be alright. Do you think we will catch the thieves before it is too late?"

"It will never be too late. We will succeed. We will kill them one by one until they give us the Key. Now let's get started!"

Merm took the lead. They all went down the path. Slowly the torch light was absorbed by the dark of the cave. It was only a matter of when, not where they would find the thieves. Since crossing the Falls of Light they were now on their own. There could be no more influence from the image of Merm's and Rmont's dreams.

- - - - - - - - - - - - - - - - - -

"Impossible! How did you allow them to pass!"

"I gave them the knowledge."

"You W H A T ! They are beyond our control now. What will stop them from using the magic for their own gain?"

"They think of me as an ally. They will want my guidance after they return from the zone, and they do not know of the *Passwords*, only the Key. They will be limited just as the one before. I will convince them to use the power to unknowingly transfer the magic to me. They will be easily fooled. Their greed for more magic will be their undoing."

"Each time we speak there are newer complications. I grow tired of the excuses."

"There has been other magic at work against me. Every occasion is matched or undermined by it. I cannot be expected to bring fast results when I must deal with the unpredictable. You have not warned me of the traps left behind! You of all others, should have known of these!"

"Yes. Those were not expected even by me. I thought that they no longer existed, or if they did, were too long in disuse to be of any threat. There are things that even I was not privy to in those times. Let us hope that is all of the tricks left by our predecessors"

"All we can do now is wait for the next opportunity, and try to weaken the Magic further from outside the zone."

"Yes. That might prove of some help to your two Gotts. I will do whatever I can."

"Thank you Wakan. We are only shortly delayed, but we will have the *Passwords*. Then we will control all the Magic and the Balance for all time. Let these worlders have their moment. It will be their last. I guarantee it."

"It will either be *their* or *your* last moment. If you understand my meaning."

Dorluc didn't respond. Wakan faded into the void. He did not like threats. He would have to deal with Wakan sooner than he thought.

Chapter 11.

Deep beneath the surface ruins were a series of labyrinths and caverns, all interconnected and leading to the central place of the Magic. Here lay the bones of the Old Ones. All along the inner tunnels were their crypts. It was to this inner sanctum, that the Key with the *Passwords* was to be delivered, and it was here that all must pass in order to reach their final destination: the *Keeper of Three*. Only when placed within the ancient hand of this first Keeper's grasp would the worlds be safe.

The crypts were in narrow tunnels, with no particular order, size, or placement, along the carved out rock wall tombs. Some of these box-like holes were empty, others full of cobwebs and bugs, but most still displayed the dusty old remains of what were once strong and magical individuals. There was no writing or illustration upon the free space of these walls. Just silence! A silence so still that chills ran down your spine.

The skulls and bones were almost alive, and at any instant it seemed as if one from behind would sit upright and question the intrusion of any who passed. There was also a sense of being watched. Here, undisturbed for generations, the physical proof of the existence of the Old Ones lay. Only the moles within those Chosen and the shared consciousness of all the Chosen before, remembered this place. All others were gone.

The ruins above were a ruse! The Old Ones had kept the existence of their underground home secret and far from the wandering eyes of those not of the three. It was the seat of all their wisdom and Magic. From here they could protect the Balance and remain undetected. But all was quiet now, and their secret exposed. They did not expect that one of their own would reveal the knowledge to others!

The Crypts of TIKA

Merm, Rmont and Gorg, had continued their exploration of the tunnel passage from the Falls of Light. They had not rested long in the cavern beyond the falls' door. They were unaware of time. The urgency to find the thieves sped them on! Up and down they walked, sometimes in very narrow and low passages. They stuck close together, seeing only as far ahead or behind as their light permitted. Though each was prepared for some sort of encounter nothing was mentioned by any out loud. They walked on determined and silent. By the time they had reached the labyrinths of crypts, they were ready to welcome any sight that might indicate that they were approaching some end to this otherwise boundless tunnel of darkness.

"Who bones be?" Gorg was unnerved by the sight and musty smell of the decay.

"This must be the crypt of the city. I would say that we are below Tika. What do you think?" Merm projected his words at Rmont. He still disliked and did not trust the Rider.

"Yes. This must be their sacred burial place. I don't mind saying that it feels uncomfortable!"

"Don't be a fool. These are just the worn out bones of the ones of this once great place."

"Where are we to go from here?"

"I don't know, but we'll just keep going until we come to some sort of exit or...just keep your eyes open for anything!" Merm hoped to himself that they were in time to catch the thieves.

"Is there no mention of this place in the Forbidden Books?" Rmont wanted something that could give them a better idea of what to expect. The writing on the box had pointed out a destination, the Keeper of Tika. But, there were other scribblings that Merm and Rmont had not understood. These held important meaning.

"There is only a vague reference," Merm stopped walking and pondered the fourth of the Forbidden Books. He searched his recollection of them, "Yes, there was an allusion to the place where all is *kept*. Under the great place lies hidden the seed."

"What does it mean?"

"There was more. 'High on the pedestal the revered remain. All will flow from its source.'

There must be an ending to this place. That is where we must go."

"Is there any other mentioning in the Books?"

"No. Just...yes...'Follow the passage of decay.' This must be that passage!" Merm was pleased that this knowledge had returned to him at a time of need. It was as if a weight was lifting, a darkness that had dulled his abilities to remember such things; a deep

memory of a freer 'self' that had been submerged long
ago by someone or something! He was feeling re-
freshed and unfettered, like long ago when he was
younger and just starting his climb to power.

"Go let us. No like this place!" Gorg, who had been
examining some of the tombs while Rmont and Merm
spoke, was growing more impatient and agitated.

"It is a little eerie. You're right. We need to find
the place where this box belongs; the place where the
thieves will take the Key." Merm tapped the concealed box quietly. Rmont was too preoccupied with
the present surroundings to notice the movement.

They went on, trying not to look at the hideousness
of the remains within the crypt. The tunnel grew from
narrow to wide. The height also began to slowly increase to the point where the two Gotts could now
comfortably stand fully upright. Then the tunnel appeared to end, in a dark black wall! Carefully they
approached. No, it was a turn, a sharp ninety degree
corner. Merm walked ahead and pushed the light forward. There were cobwebs and bugs hanging from the
tombs. As they walked they had to duck in places to
avoid colliding with the ancient spinnings. Gorg hated
this. He pushed the webs away with his arms. The
webs were strong and thick, and in some cases the
bones that supported them broke away as well. They
were brittle with age. All of a sudden, one of the
skeletons from an upper tomb partially fell from its
resting place, pulled by the web being cleared away by
Gorg. A piece of a porous bony hand seemed to grasp
Gorg's left shoulder. Gorg screamed in his startlement
and turned to come face to face with a the skull that
owned the outstretched hand. Gorg's screech drew the
rapid nervous attention of Merm and Rmont.

"What the...!" either Merm or Rmont exclaimed.
Instantly they saw the reason for Gorg's fright.

"It's only a few bones! Are Riders always so
edgy?" Merm was cutting to Gorg.

"Bad place is! I first go." Ignoring the comment

Gorg pushed by them, grabbed the light from Merm and went ahead in a huff! Merm and Rmont privately enjoyed the release this made of their own apprehension of this place. They followed behind.

The tunnel continued to expand and the floor slightly to rise. There was a sense of light ahead. A dim green. They each focused upon its hint of existence. As they moved, the ceiling lifted far above their heads, and the walls, fell away as they entered a large cavernous room. A dim green light exuded from the walls, causing their starved eyes to squint. When they became used to the luminous glow, they stood together and took in the complete sight.

It was an anti-chamber of sorts, which had no tombs in the walls. Where the light emitted, was the same strange plant as was found under the ground in Norkleau. It was old. In certain areas there were no plants illuminating, but pictures and writings. Everything about the room was rustic, except the sophistication of the wall carvings. On the other side of the room was an exit. All three walked into the center of this space, and looked upon the carvings. The ceiling was full of masterful work.

"Can you understand what is written? Is it the same as the ones in Norkleau?" Rmont questioned his Lord.

Merm examined and paused, "It is of the same origin, but older. I can understand some, not all. It is a history of the ones who built this place. It tells of their purpose and of a great Magic, a secret, a balance for all. It tells of three. Yes there is much mention of three. Three is linked to the Magic. I don't understand how, but it seems that three controls or maintains something."

"What does it control?" Rmont was paying more attention to Merm and ignoring Gorg who was now sitting upon the floor disinterested.

"What here come for? Picture no profit!" Gorg thought out loud.

"It doesn't say," Merm was too absorbed to hear

Gorg, "It speaks of a...I'm not certain. It directs all of the three to enter. It doesn't make sense. It speaks of the power and Magic within. Of a unity of strength. It is very powerful."

"Then we must be careful upon entering the other side. There must be a great source ahead. Is there any danger?" Rmont was trying to piece it all together.

"A warning. Only those of the purest three can act, or can access whatever lies beyond this room. I can't make out the other symbols."

"Then we are almost there! We are at the place where the thieves will come. The Key must unlock this Magic, here. They must have discovered its use and have come to unleash upon themselves this great power. We must get the Key and unleash that power on us!" Rmont's eyes were bulging from his lust and nearness to acquiring such invincibility.

"Maybe already are. Maybe we late be," Gorg sobered both Rmont and Merm who felt so close to success that they could taste it.

"It is possible that there was another way, but I don't think they are here yet. They are probably just behind. We have been pursuing and haven't rested long. They are probably not feeling threatened or rushed. They will become careless and give us an advantage by wasting time." Merm was accessing, by reflex, his skill as a tactician and a veteran survivor. He felt intuitively that his general analysis, if not the detail, was inherently correct.

"What will they do?"

"Rmont, you worry too much. They will come and 'we' will be waiting. 'We' will not let them take this moment from us." Merm was feeling different as he spoke. He was remembering the early times when he and Rmont had worked against his political enemies and how united together, taken the leadership of the Gott. He was sensing a return to older meanings of we, ones that only included Rmont and himself, not this Rider. Rmont seemed to understand the tone of

Merm's words and welcomed their meaning! It was strange.

"That has been my duty from the beginning of our careers." Merm understood to what Rmont was referring.

"Then go must now. No chance take. No want miss like at water." Gorg was right. No matter how skilled Merm was, there was always the unpredictable element. No-one could control that!

After a few more surveys of the room and pictures, with Gorg in the lead, they crossed the room proceeding into the opposite tunnel. Once more came the dark narrow path. Again the two Gotts were forced to stoop over as they progressed. There were not as many tombs on this side of the tunnel. In fact the farther they went the fewer they encountered. Eventually there was nothing but the smooth rock. They kept in motion. Inside himself, Merm knew that the end was very close.—Soon he would have *all* that he ever wanted!

Time was meaningless inside the canyons that housed the Southworlders. Julian had fallen into secure sleep and felt fully rested upon awakening. They were still in the twilight of the dim green plants, when Julian was spoken to:

"Julian. Julian. The time is near. You must listen carefully to what must now be heard." The voice seemed to be coming from somewhere within the area, but it was not of Darla or his nephews. It was the voice, amongst many, of his father.

"Father?" Julian thought he was awake and speaking out loud. He couldn't comprehend why the others were not disturbed. They just slept. "Father is that you?"

"Yes. Listen. Do not speak now." The opaque image of his father was in front of him. It wore the traditional garb of the Stonemason's of Jard. Julian did not question but awaited his father's words.

"You are not alone here. There are others who seek that which you are charged to protect. There is nothing that can be done to stop them. They have been given powerful knowledge from the *Evil* side of the Balance. You must go quickly to the first of us all. He lies past the tunnels of decay, at the crest of the fulcrum. It is at the end of the last tunnel, after the Cavern of Three. Together there, you can access the magic that you will need to reach the Keeper. Past the Keeper is another passage. It leads to the canyons outside and opens to a great sudden abyss to the waters below. You must not allow the others to possess the Key or the *Passwords*. Place the Books into that which was once a hand, and now is a cage of bones. Hold the Key and all chant the tune. The Key must be thrown freely into the watery abyss, no touch must be upon it as it enters the river below, only then will the Balance be safe!"

"What if those others get in the way and prevent me from getting to the Keeper?"

"Use the powers to fool their perception." Julian had forgotten his newest trick! "They *must* not prevail! It is our, your calling: a Keeper of the Key and Stoneman's son. Do what is necessitated."

"I don't understand all that has happened?"

"There is no time now. We will again speak. Wake the others and go. May the power of the Three fill you!" With that the image, as before, faded. There was nothing Julian could do to prolong the visit. He would follow his father's bidding. He was a Stoneman, a Keeper of the Key!

Julian woke the others without telling them of his vision or communication with his father. They had slept long enough. The final stage of their journey was about to begin. He wondered briefly how it would all turn out.

"Not already! I could sleep much longer." Eruinn

was grumpy.

"Me too!" echoed Thiunn.

"We must get to TIKA as fast as we can." Julian added to his shaking of each of them.

"Yes, the *Evil* cannot be too far from us. The last thing we want is to run into them down here!" Darla was ready to continue what she felt was the last leg of the journey. How welcome it would be to return home and not worry any more of the *Evil* threat!

"Uncle J, I feel very safe here. It's like I've been here before. I sense that I know we are near, though I can't quite see it clearly." Eruinn was looking for re-inforcement of this new awareness.

"All of us have. The ones that lie within are from this place. Since we are blended amongst them we also sense their shared feelings. In a sense we will always be here and not. But we can speak more of these changes after we have accomplished the tasks at hand." He faced them all: "I will go first. Stay close together, and we will arrive safely."

They threw their bags over their shoulders and went on into the tunnel. With each step nearer, the moles within each of them continued to be more awakened and grew stronger in their remembrances of this place. They were very close to the source.

The tunnel that they were in was approaching Tika from the south, unlike Merm's party who had come from the south east. All of the passages were narrow dark places, but Darla, Eruinn, Thiunn and Julian had the surefootedness brought by the inner knowledge of this old familiarity. In previous times they had all been here frequently.

- - - - - - - - - - - - - - - - -

The passages under and throughout the canyons were pathways for the Old Ones to come and go unnoticed by other's eyes. Just like the passageways around Norkleau and the Lake of Choices, they

weaved in and out, all eventually linking with one another. It was completely possible to make the entire
journey through the north by underground passage.
This added greatly to all the myths of the Magic of the
Old Ones, particularly the way in which they appeared
and disappeared without a trace. The whereabouts of
these secret passages was almost forgotten, except for
the few that Darla, and now the others had rediscov-
ered.

Originally the luminous vegetation had lined every
tunnel. It required little attention and thrived in the
environment of these places. Occasionally the plants
were tended and re-grafted onto the rock, but that
wasn't needed too often. Over the ages, since the Old
Ones had passed on, much of the vegetation had perished through disease, age and neglect. The energy
they absorbed from the passersby within the tunnels
and caves, could last an average life span. This is
what caused them to shine their bright green light.
That light slowly dimmed until recharged by the
proximity of the usually frequent travelers. Since the
departure of the Old Ones, only minimal energy was
left to flow through the labyrinths. It was enough to
maintain an existence and the dimmest of a glow.
With the shifts and changes caused by Dorluc to the
Balance over the ages, some areas had become starved
of the revitalizing energy and the plants had perished,
leaving those areas of the underground world in total
blackness. Julian and the others internally understood
this. There was a sadness amongst the many consciousnesses inside them for this loss. Those times
were long ago gone. The times of the beauty and
magic, the ways of goodness and harmony with all.

- - - - - - - - - - - - - - - - - -

On through the tunnels they progressed. Jewel was
emitting a constant bright light through each of its
gems which threw off colorful beams of light through-

out the tunnel. Darla had never witnessed such a show from her companion!

Thiunn, being the closest asked, "Darla, why does Jewel sparkle so?"

"We must be approaching a great source of Magic. Its energy is being absorbed by Jewel and these are the results of the power. We are also showing signs of the effect of this Magic: the déjà vu, the sensing within and awareness."

"Will we ever return to the quiet of before, or will we always be this way?"

"I don't know. I have never gone through this. What is happening now, the threat and disturbances to the worlds, has rekindled a Magic that has been long in disuse. We are involved and must go wherever it leads and accept whatever we become. It is a calling." Thiunn fell back to walking and silence. Darla wondered at what the results would be.

The tunnel began to rise upward and expand in size. After a long silent march, a sharp turn and then a more level passage they came to a wider tunnel. This tunnel was different. In its walls were holes, the size of coffins. Row upon row existed in all shapes, placement and sizes. Cobwebs dangled. This was another tunnel of decay.

Julian stopped and spoke out loud to himself, "The passage of decay. The Crypts of Tika. We are here! Do not disturb a thing. These are the remains of the ones before."

They entered and observed in silence the curiosity and horror of the spectacle. It went on with hundreds of carved out tombs. Eruinn was squeamish. Thiunn pretended bravado. Darla pushed them both along and down the tunnel to catch up with Julian, who had picked up his pace and was farther ahead.

"There is an opening here!" Julian could just make it out, "It looks like the entrance to a large room. There's a dim light, like the passages at the lake."

He was correct. Within a few more paces they all stood amidst the dim green glow in the same place that Merm, Rmont and Gorg had found not long before. *The Cavern of Three!*

Julian appreciated where they had arrived. This was the place for which his father's image had prepared him, where they could acquire the Magic needed to return the Key and the *Passwords* to the Keeper.

The room was large and held many of the hieroglyphics of the other caves of which they were all familiar. The only difference was the deliberate referencing to three. Like the other caves at the Lake of Choices and Norkleau, there was the same general type of symbol in an arch shape; one in the pivot position and the others one to the left, one right and one above. A thin prismatic line extended below the pivot symbol. That was the only difference. That, and the reference of the number.

Julian began to feel more changed. Like the others, he noted that the consciousness within was now becoming more dominant over his mortal being. His 'self' was watching while the other consciousnesses directed. There was no fear. They were benevolent and old. Their experience stretched as far back as the original ones who had been first chosen. As 'his' essence mingled, the depth of the emotions and knowledge of them was astounding, and beyond the ability to be expressed by normal words.

"This is an old place to which we have returned." Darla's dominance spoke, "It is good to be alive and with friends!" The oldest communing was initiated.

"With friends," all answered.

It was an unusual phenomenon. They were all still the same in look and sound, even in familiarity. Darla was still Darla, Eruinn and Thiunn still themselves and Julian, Julian. But they weren't! They had each taken on more. Maybe this was who they all individually really were, and the other simpler selves, the strangers. They were closer, and more intimate in their sense of one another, intuitively quick and determined. They knew where they were and why. They knew what must be done and how.

"'D' give me Jewel so that we may finish what has been started." Julian affectionately spoke to Darla.

"A moment. It has been so long since I felt you around me. Come. Hold me once again. I have longed for your caress," Darla held out her arms. Julian moved and embraced his mate."

"Don't you two ever stop!" Thiunn was embarrassed.

"It has been a long time." Eruinn silenced his brother to allow the distant loves to sparkle a moment in their union.

"We must continue," Julian held her.

Reluctantly releasing, Darla whispered, "I love you."

Julian felt a tinge so deep within that he was unable to speak. He gazed into the beautiful eyes before him and, letting go, sobered his mind to the present. Darla gave him the sword as he withdrew.

"It has been long since our last reawakening. There is greater darkness this time. Let us hope Jewel can provide what we need." He crossed to the symbol by the passage and was about to place Jewel in its place amongst the arched figures, when Eruinn noticed:

"Look. We are not alone. Some others have passed through not long ago!"

On the ground were the footprints of Merm and his company. These were fresh disturbances upon the ground and led into the far tunnel.

- - - - - - - - - - - - - - - - - - -

The fine trackers that they were, the three were fast to determine whether anyone else had come along this way before them. They were pleased to discover that theirs were the only marks that were recently made.

"Shouldn't we hide our own tracks, in case the

thieves are behind?"

"Gorg do."

"No it is not necessary," Merm cared not to waste the effort, "The darkness of the tunnel will conceal our passing. They will not think to observe such things. Remember, as far as they are concerned, we are behind and chasing after them!"

"What if they do see them?"

"They won't. Even if they do, they can't stop. They must come this way. There is no other tunnel."

"That's what we thought at the Falls."

"This is different. Believe me this is the only way!" Merm's voice slightly raised. This informed Rmont, and Gorg not to question the Lord of the Gotts again!

It had become evident to Merm that their final destination was not on the surface, but here in these caverns. Realizing this, he would pursue what he felt was at the end of this, or the next passageway. He was not interested in the opinion of Rmont, and especially not the Rider! He sped off, taking the light. Rmont and Gorg had no option but to follow quickly or be left behind in the dark.

Merm was also preoccupied with the changes that were coming to his attention. He seemed rejuvenated, as if a weight was being lifted and he was obliging to no-one! He was unable to determine the cause, but coupled with the excitement of this chase and the imminent success to his journey, he was greatly pleased. Yet, at the same time, moody.

Along the tunnel they maneuvered themselves, not knowing what to expect. There was a hint of freshness in the air. A slight breeze was blowing onto them. They came to a fork in the tunnel. Which way should they go? Merm decided to split them up. Gorg would go left, and Rmont accompany him going to the right. Gorg, suspicious of all Gotts was not interested in this plan of splitting up!

"Gorg you stay. No go."

"You will do as I order." Merm displayed little patience.

Rmont, suspecting the real reason for Gorg's hesitation, interrupted what would soon develop into a fight, saying: "There is plenty of profit for us all, but we cannot go in two directions at once unless we separate. We will not abandon our brave Rider friend."

"What if nothing find?"

"Then come back and join us ahead, wherever this path leads. We will mark the way if there are other forks."

Gorg thought, "Okay."

The crisis was avoided. Gorg would go left and they right. There was no other logical route to follow. Rmont handed him the other smaller torch, after lighting it with the larger one in Merm's grasp. He accepted it, and mumbled as he entered his part of the fork.

The tunnel to the left was more narrow than the Rider expected. Its walls were jagged but plain. Gorg felt uneasy by himself. He was not afraid. He just felt as if there was another presence behind him. The tunnel began to climb, for about thirty lengths and then leveled out to continue it's course. On this higher level there was a stronger current of fresher air. An opening of some sort was in the vicinity. Carefully Gorg progressed, not wanting to carelessly come across an ancient booby trap, or lose his light. Still, there was the presence that he sensed near to him.

"Who there is!" He could take no more, turning around to confront the invisible force. There was no reply, just the sound of the breeze as it ricocheted off the tunnel rock. "Who there. Make known." Getting no response, Gorg, resumed his forward motion. He slowed once or twice more thinking he could quickly turn and confront whatever it was. Each time there was nothing.

Rmont and Merm had a larger tunnel, similar to the one that exited the Cavern of Three. There was no dramatic change in direction or level, but the breeze in this tunnel was strong and fresh. Unnerved by the prospect of total darkness they each took turns trying to shelter the torch as it flickered in the breeze. The farther along they went the stronger the breeze became. It was more and more difficult to keep the torch from being extinguished. Then an unexpected dip in the tunnel ceiling bumped Merm's forehead. He dropped the torch. They were left in the blackness of the tunnel!

"Lord where are you? Are you hurt?"

"Right here!" Merm stretched out his hand and touched Rmont, who immediately latched onto Merm's arm.

"Hold my arm. We will go on." Rmont examined the blackness, "There look. We can follow that glimmer ahead."

In the brightness of the torch, neither had seen the faint light ahead. In the black it shone like a beacon. They made their way slowly toward it. It grew as they approached.

The tunnel brightened and Gorg found himself walking out onto a ledge into yet another cavern. This room was smaller than the one before and a brightness filled it, as well as a fresh breeze from a passage to his left, which he assumed was the source of this radiance from the outside world. It shined in and spotlighted a shrine in the center of the room. The shrine stood centrally upon a raised dais. It was simple, just a stone pedestal and a large container made of stone. There were the hieroglyphics of the other caverns carved into it and from his elevation he could see more bones inside its lidless rectangular shape.

There was another cavity off to his right beneath his ledge, similar to the one he had exited, and he could make out the loud voices of the two Gotts, as they drew closer from their path. It was not long before they both appeared, a little dazed by the suddenness of the bright yellow light, and the ominous quality of the place. Merm was gently rubbing his forehead.

"What so long take!? Wait have I!" Gorg took pleasure in this chance to make a jab at Merm, who now had two lumps to soothe.

The Gotts both responded with dirty looks. "Come down here! We will need your help," Rmont ordered.

Gorg considered, then got to his knees and gradually slid over the side of the ledge till his outstretched arms dangled him two lengths from the lower level. He let go and landed safely.

"Good. Now, what have we here." Merm was content to be back in charge.

"This seems to be a shrine of sorts. There is writing on the sarcophagus." Rmont saw that this was an inner tomb of someone important. "It has similar symbols as in the caverns."

"They are very old. They welcome in the name of three, and warn others to go back." Merm had come closer to the dais and stopped.

"What type warning be?" Gorg wasn't about to take any chances, so he backed off.

"Death. Yes death! Those not with the three, whatever that is, will perish if...I can't make out the rest," Merm was puzzled.

"Certainly this is only a scare tactic! How could anything happen." Rmont, fed up with the mystery approached and stepped up on the dais. A high tone sounded. "More theatrics!" He leaned over about to touch the stone of the coffin, when a beam of light fell from the ceiling and froze him in place. He could speak but not move. Slowly the beam spred outward. Merm and Gorg were stunned, it had all happened without warning.

"Help me! Something's got hold of me!" Rmont was scared.

Before the other two could answer there came a gravely heavy rolling sound.

"Look! Tunnels blocked." Gorg saw the huge piece

of rock close in mechanically upon itself. "Only there not blocked!" He pointed out the passage from which the breeze and outside light was coming.

"Don't leave me!" Rmont sensed that they were about to try to escape the encroaching beam by way of the bright passage.

Merm signaled to Gorg to run for the other passage: "Sorry Rmont, each for himself."

"You --------!" The sound of the closing rock in the tunnels muffled the word.

Gorg and Merm ran down the short passage. There would be no turning back! The beam was filling the tomb rapidly. The screams of Rmont reached their ears. Such agony! They reached the opening of the passage, which was to the outside. It was bright out. The opening was a round hole in the canyon wall, high up. Far, far below, looking like a trickle, was a tributary of the Pass river. There was no way out!

"No jump can. Too far. What do?" Gorg was stumped.

"If that beam doesn't stop we may have to just take our chances!" Merm tried to gauge whether or not the billowing beam was still flowing their way or if it was slowing.—Neither! It had merely been filling the cavity within. Now that it was full, it was picking up speed and overflowing in their direction. What a way to end!

"No want die! Help us!" Gorg was not sure if he should stand in front of Merm and between the beam, or behind and between the abyss! He didn't trust either. The pressure was getting to him and it was irritating the anxious Merm.

"Stop whining you fool! Be quiet or I will toss you over the side before me!" Both of them were slowly stepping backwards, keeping as much distance as they safely could from the beam. There wasn't much space left to tread! There was nowhere to go. Merm could see no escape!

- - - - - - - - - - - - - - - - - - -

"Foot prints. Large ones. Lord Merm is here! He must have obtained great knowledge to get here so soon! He has acquired powerful allies." Darla was crouched over studying the marks.

"There is no more time to waste." Julian turned back to replace Jewel. As it clicked in, the multi tone melody played, and after a low rolling noise, another tunnel just to the right of the present one opened .

- - - - - - - - - - - - - - - - - -

Just when all seemed lost and they were teetering over the brink, the beam vanished and the tunnels un-blocked. They were saved! But how and why? Coming back to their sensing and remembering all that had occurred inside, Merm called out, "Rmont!" and ran back through the passage into the tomb. Rmont was gone!

As Gorg came in, nothing was said. Merm felt an emptiness, but quickly disguised his remorse.

"It is too bad. He was a good friend." That was all to Rmont's epitaph.

"What now do?"

"We wait for the thieves. We have paid the price for the right to the Key."

They both kept their distance from the dais and backed toward the lower tunnel opening.

"We will need a place to hide, but what entrance will they enter by?" Merm was thinking out loud. If they chose the wrong place to hide, the thieves would be alerted and perhaps escape. There was also the consideration that the same events that had just tran-spired might be repeated. In that case, Merm and Gorg would be happier on the other side of any block-ade and beam! There was also the chance that the thieves would split up, as they had done. Then there would be no safe hiding! Finally, Merm decided to take the upper tunnel with Gorg. They would have to gamble on that choice. Gorg helped Merm to climb the ledge and then in turn was pulled up. They sat on the ledge to catch their breath. How long they would have to wait was uncertain, but they could not turn around now and retreat with tails between their legs.

- - - - - - - - - - - - - - - - - -

Their tunnel was straight and smooth. Its door had been activated by the placement of Jewel within the symbols... A lock of sorts. Not only did it release this door, but it also shut off the guardianship within the tomb of the Keeper. This was the reason why Merm and Gorg had been saved. Unfortunately once caught in its force, it was too late for Rmont. His life source was returned to the Balance. None of this was known to Julian as he had placed Jewel. It was just good timing on the part of Merm and Gorg!

They arrived at the end of the tunnel. Another rock door was in front of them and like all these doors the four symbols were placed at eye height awaiting the correct sequence which played the tune to unleash its mechanism. They all stopped.

"This is it. On the other side there could be anything. Once the door is opened we must act with speed. Eruinn and Thiunn, it will be your job to hold off Merm and whoever is with him. He must not get in the way of my duty. I must reach the Keeper and place the Books within his grasp. When this is done, Darla and I will chant the Tune of Balance. Then the Key must be thrown into the river from the canyon passage opening. Until the Key is submerged in its depths the Balance will be vulnerable.

"Uncle Julian. Maybe no-one is there?"

"Thiunn, that would be the best situation, but I sense that there is some *Evil* there."

"We've been through worse, right?" Darla tried to reduce the tension. Eruinn and Thiunn felt minimally comforted.

This was to be a united effort. Through this pooling

of their magic they would be a mighty foe. However, they were uncertain, and that could cause them enough distraction and weaken their use of the Magic.

Just as Julian was to proceed and open the door, a soft voice emanated amongst them. They all listened as each of their names was uttered.

"Do not allow doubt to weaken your bonds. The *Evil* will use this to divide you all. The Three will keep you strong. Rely on them. Together you will intensify. Use the Three."

The mentioning of the number was a mystery to them. They tried to find some deeper meaning, but were not able to understand. What was this Three other than some religion or philosophy? Perhaps there was something that they each had missed? They could not make the connection, and for good reason. This knowledge of Three was very privileged. Even amongst the select group of Old Ones who had become aware of the greater mysteries of the Magic of the world. In itself, it remained harmless. In the unscrupulous hands of *Evil*, the outcome even for them was not clear. It was very unstable and delicate. In order to completely assure its integrity, it was never incorporated into the multiple awareness of the moles of the Chosen.

The secrets of the existence and use of the Magic of 'Three', were kept in the *Passwords of Promise*. If placed in the wrong minds, they could affect the Balance for all time. The Old Ones had learned that such discoveries were to be left hidden. Even they could never hope to fully unravel the fabric that bound everything together. The slightest aberration would cause an irreversible chain of events. It was, therefore, imperative that such knowledge be returned and placed into safe keeping far from the *Evil* side of the Balance. The *Evil* wasn't sure of the level of power that these 'Passwords' contained. They did know that there was something, but that was the limit of their wisdom. Julian must not allow the *Passwords* to be taken, or the Key that would unlock their Magic, found. Somehow along the way, the knowledge of the Magic of these *Passwords* had been discovered, but until recently their whereabouts was unknown.

The Chosen Ones had been given the task to rout out such searchers of this knowledge and dissuade them. The Stonemen were Keepers of the hiding of the *Passwords*. It had been a good method until their existence had been discovered. A discovery that led, during the reign of Ho and the Separation Wars, to the almost complete extermination of all of the Chosen. Only the most dormant had survived.

Somehow greater magic than was possible from the inhabitants of the regular worlds, was being used by creatures that should not have been privy to such wonders. On the other side of the rock door there could be some of these poor creatures, who were not totally cognizant to the real purpose of their exploitation by the *Evil* side of the Balance. Julian and his party were about to find out!

"Ready?" Julian took a breath, "On the count of three. One, two..."

Chapter 12.

"**I** have not been able to see them once they entered the zone. It is not clear to me what has happened. My magic cannot locate them." Dorluc was puzzled.

"This is not good. There is much change. They are in the tunnels and approach the One."

"It could not be foreseen. Their magic together is powerful. They have tapped its oldest parts. There is nothing we can do."

"There is something I will do!" Waken's image faded from sight as the last three words lingered on.

- - - - - - - - - - - - - - - - - -

Merm and Gorg were silently sitting on the ledge as Julian, from behind the rock said 'three'. The symbols were pressed and the melody of unlocking sounded. This time the tune was heard on both sides of the rock.

"What be?" Gorg jumped up.

"Quickly hide wherever you can." As Merm spoke the rock door, which was opposite and below began to slowly open. "There," he pointed, "They come!"

There was an eeriness to the cavern. Its cool dark walls seemed to be alighting with some sort of strange energy. It flowed all around and there was a slight hint of a tune that seemed to be emanating from the direction of the dais that held the rectangular coffin. As the rock walls began to glow there was also the beginning of a distant strength of energy. It was old and omnipresent! These were just the feelings that Merm and Gorg instantly felt at the moment of the opening of the hidden door by the thieves. There was a stirring in the Magic, that was coming from this place! It would welcome the Chosen but punish all others.

As Thiunn and Julian had pressed the symbols together, Darla and Eruinn prepared for whatever might be on the other side. The door opened slowly and they all crouched in ready position. There was the bright shaft of light from the outside, and the dais, and silence. They did not notice the glow amidst the walls, being overcome by the sudden brightness of the outside tunnel of light.

Standing for a moment to sense the room, Julian broke in, "Quickly. Now is the chance." He felt they were clear and that there was no time to waste. There was a new strength to all of them. A strength that was part of the Magic. Now in these last few moments the rising up of their inner moles was complete. They all were aware together in their knowledge of their past and present. This was home.

"How nice it is to be back," Darla softly spoke after they all had entered the cavern and begun to adjust to the light.

"Yes, it has been a long time," Julian remembered, "but we must act quickly," he turned to face the dais and coffin, "there is our destination."

Merm and Gorg. who had not yet been spotted, watched from overhead, as these four issued into the room. When they saw that one male thief and the female were going to mount the dais, they prepared to make an escape into the passageways. Nothing happened! There was no closing of the entrances, nor the energy that had gripped Rmont, nor the cloud that had threatened them. They, nervously waiting, prepared to run from the cavern into the safety of the passageway.

Julian stepped unto the dais with Darla, keeping a watchful eye. He took the *Passwords of Promise* from their hiding place in his cloak. Untying the twine that bound them together, he moved forward and peered down into the coffin. '*The Keeper*,' he thought. He knelt before the edifice and mumbled indistinguishable words that were half melodic in sound. When he had finished, he turned his head to Darla showing a smile. He felt reassured that he could continue and complete the task. He rose up and placed the books gently amongst the bones that were once a hand. Remarkably the bones held together as he touched them. They seemed to rise up a little and seemed to grasp hold of the *Passwords*.

After they had been placed, Julian backed away a step. Merm and Gorg watched on amazed. Darla joined Julian in front of the coffin. They both stood still for a moment. Julian then removed the Key from its hiding place in his clothing. Holding it up in front of his forehead with his right hand, he presented it to the Keeper. As he performed this ceremony, he indicated to the others that they should now join him. Eruinn and Thiunn stepped forward and stood together with Darla. They all stood with their backs to Merm! The chant of old began:

"Ic noon vra ba, houn gre juk!"

It was in the oldest tongue. The language of the Old Ones. The Stoneman found himself watching from outside his body as others controlled, or shared their essence within him. He was not afraid. He knew it was meant to be. It was all part of the calling as a Keeper of Three. He watched as he also led the chant. Darla and the nephews copied his words after they had been spoken. There began a deep rumbling in the cavern.

This was the opportunity for Merm and Gorg to surprise them and take the Key! They decided to wait no longer for the correct opportunity. As the Southworlders finished their chant, Merm and Gorg slid down the ledge to the floor, where Merm blurted: "Give me *my* Key!"

Eruinn and Thiunn were the first to turn around and see Merm. They threw up their hands as if to project something. Gorg who was staying off to the side of

Merm ducked. Merm began to use his magic in a reflex action, and a tremendous struggle of Magic and power between them began.

Merm projected a thought of equalization. It struck the thoughts of the nephews and now they all began the struggle of the two sides of the Magic! Back and forth they went, hurling their best magical energy. Soon the three of them were stalemated in place. Merm was not able to overpower the two.

Darla had jumped down from the dais to attack the Rider, and yelled at Julian : "Go! With the Key!" She indicated that he should dispose of the Key as he was meant to, while he could still access the outside tunnel!

Julian knew he must hurry. He turned to check the books that he had placed within the bones. They were gone! All that remained were ashes, but they weren't the ashes of the books! There was no time to consider. He turned and ran into the tunnel that housed the shaft of light.

The sighting of the Key in Julian's grip, gave Merm more incentive to win his magical battle with the two youngsters. He focused his greed and anger. Suddenly he felt stronger as if another had stepped into his soul. His ability to use his magic increased, and with his new strength suddenly felt the winning advantage. He began to feel a compulsion, one that had always been there unnoticed by his conscious mind, until recently, since he had found the Key in Norkleau! He was no longer in control of himself. He realized this now, and accepted it. He suddenly knew that this strange force within him had been the same one that had helped him to his position of power. He must listen and allow himself to be its vehicle. *He had to stop the one with the Key! He must not let the Key go!*

As if it was summoned from within himself, out of nowhere materialized the same *Evil* image that had confronted Thiunn in Julian's cottage at Jard. Merm thought it was his magic. Eruinn, Thiunn and Darla knew otherwise. It was a great *Evil*! Immediately and with a vengeance, it turned its full force upon Thiunn. Thiunn called out. Eruinn would have to lessen his hold on Merm and come to the aid of his brother. Darla could not help, she was still too entrenched in combat with the Rider.

During this moment, Merm tried to draw away his magic from the struggling youngsters. With the onslaught of the *Evil* energy, Merm managed to break free. He caught a glimpse of the thief with the Key escaping into the lighted tunnel. From inside a voice demanded: '*Go after him. Get the Key!*' There was no questioning or thought of choice. He turned toward, and ran after Julian!

The struggle with the *Evil* continued until Merm was well into the passage. Then it abruptly stopped! Just as it had in Jard. Now Thiunn and Eruinn were free to help Darla.

Noticing this outnumbering, the Rider backed off his aggressive fight with Darla, and slithered into the passageway on this lower level, to get away from all the activity, and to escape this now unbalanced fight. He would remember this desertion by the Lord of the Gotts!

The three stood together. They were out of breath and under physical strain. When the realization that Merm had gone into the tunnel of light after Julian finally connected with them, Thiunn exclaimed:

"Uncle Julian! He will need our help!"

"Hurry. We can still stop that Gott!" Darla led them on and was first into the tunnel of light.

Everything was happening so quickly. The cavern was still rumbling and its walls were now glowing brightly, but the three did not have the time to notice. They all ran the short distance into and down the tunnel of light. They arrived so quickly that they almost stepped through its sudden opening and into the abyss of the canyon and river below. They stopped, and

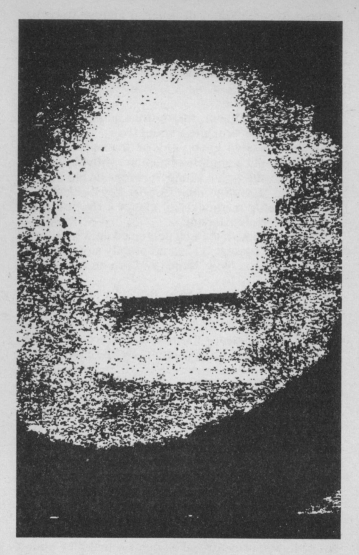

The Tunnel of Light

teetered over the edge, disoriented and not knowing what to say, or understanding what really had happened. There was no sign of a struggle, nor any clue to the fate of Merm or Julian.

They all remained silent looking over and into to the depths below. The sheer drop in every direction they searched was humbling. There was no safe way out from this tunnel! The ragged cliff walls resembled ancient mountains which were weathered and majestic. There were misty clouds hanging below, waiting to be absorbed by the magical pull of the torrid dark water beneath—a pull that even the three found hard to resist! The air was thick with moisture, and mossy vegetation clung, in a never ending struggle between barren existence or watery death, to spots on the walls. There was the faint distant sound of strong water. And far far down, resembling a stream from this height, was the mighty river! Had they fallen or been lured over?

It was a strange, colorful and bright place. It was as if Julian had jumped into the layer between the worlds of reality and magic. He felt no sensation of falling. It seemed to be a dream. He remembered running down the tunnel of light and preparing to throw the Key into the abyss, when out of nowhere he felt a hand grab, and its force make him lose his footing. As he fell into the opening, he turned his head and saw that it was Merm's body who had upset him, but they were not the same eyes! A terrifying chill, followed by a shiver, permeated his person; the hairs on his body were involuntarily standing erect!

As they passed through the opening, Merm was grabbing at the arm of Julian that led to the Key in his right hand. Julian understood. He returned his thoughts to his purpose—but it could not be done! Merm, or the *Evil* now clearly controlling, might somehow retrieve the Key! Julian tightly clenched his fist around the Key, and as he did so imagined that Merm was gone; like his episode in the river at the crossing—instantly Merm disappeared! He knew not where, but now found himself alone out of immediate danger, and in this strange formless place! A voice called out to him.

Darla searched her feelings to discover whether Julian was alive or dead. She was struck with the chilling perception of knowing what had happened. She spoke her thoughts out loud as she continued the visual search of the depths below:

"The *Evil* has returned!"